One

◇

"I bet she wears orthopedic shoes and glasses an inch thick," Jessica Wakefield told her twin sister, Elizabeth.

"You're exaggerating, Jess," Elizabeth replied calmly, reaching into her locker for her books. "She'll probably be really nice."

"Nice? Not a chance," Jessica scoffed. "The Hairnet wouldn't pick a *nice* student-teacher. She probably picked someone who gives more homework than she does."

"More homework? I hope not," Elizabeth said, getting a little worried. "I spent almost two hours last night on Mrs. Arnette's assignment."

"*Tons* more homework," Jessica predicted

as the girls headed for their next class—social studies with Mrs. Arnette, whom they liked to call "the Hairnet."

Elizabeth smiled. She knew it was just like Jessica to blow things out of proportion. Elizabeth knew her twin well, but she was always amazed at how she and Jessica could look so much alike, yet have such different personalities. They both had long blond hair and blue-green eyes, and each had a dimple in her left cheek. But Elizabeth was the more serious and responsible twin. She liked school and worked hard to earn good grades. She enjoyed being the editor of Sweet Valley Middle School's newspaper, *The Sweet Valley Sixers*, and she loved to read, especially mysteries written by Amanda Howard.

Jessica, on the other hand, read mostly fashion magazines. Her favorite activities were shopping and gossiping with the Unicorns, a group of the most popular girls in school. The Unicorns thought they were special—they had even chosen purple as their favorite color because it was the color of royalty. In Elizabeth's opinion, though, the Unicorns were mostly royal pains. In fact, she had nicknamed them the Snob Squad.

As Elizabeth followed Jessica into the classroom, she saw that her closest friend, Amy Sutton, was already there. Amy waved at Elizabeth and pointed to the front of the room. Behind the teacher's desk sat Mrs. Arnette. She looked as reserved as usual, her hair in a neat bun. But walking over to her was a tall, slender girl who looked like a model. The girl leaned over Mrs. Arnette's shoulder and began talking as she smoothed back a strand of curly blond hair. She was wearing a fuchsia zip-front shirt, tight black leggings, and funky black shoes.

"Gee, look at those orthopedic shoes, Jessica," Elizabeth whispered to her twin, barely holding back a smile.

"Come on, Lizzie, she *can't* be the student-teacher. No teacher would wear clothes as great as those!"

"Class, I'd like to introduce Ms. Shepard," Mrs. Arnette said at that moment. "She's an education major at Sweet Valley College, and she'll be your teacher for the next few weeks."

Jessica's mouth fell open. "I can't believe

she's our teacher! Don't you just love her shoes?'' she whispered to her friend Lila Fowler.

Lila nodded. "Yeah. I have a pair at home just like them."

"Yours are brown, Lila," Jessica pointed out.

"I have them in black, too," Lila said loftily. "I just haven't worn them yet because I'm still looking for the perfect outfit to go with them."

Jessica gave her friend an annoyed look. Was there anything Lila didn't own? *Probably not,* she thought. Lila's father was one of the wealthiest people in Sweet Valley, and he spoiled his daughter rotten.

"Quiet please," Mrs. Arnette said, glaring at Jessica and Lila. "While Ms. Shepard is here I will be observing from the back of the room. I want you all to give her your full cooperation. She has some interesting new ideas about education, and I'm sure you'll all benefit from her presence."

"I already am!" Aaron Dallas called out, and the class laughed.

"Well, I didn't know I could achieve such remarkable results so quickly," Ms. Shepard said, laughing. "I'll begin by telling you what we'll be studying for the next few weeks."

Jessica sighed. Mrs. Arnette had already told the class they would be learning about American pioneers—again. It seemed to Jessica that every social studies class she had ever been in had had a unit on pioneers. Not even a cool, young teacher could make that topic interesting.

"Social studies is an exciting subject," Ms. Shepard began cheerfully.

Social studies is a boring subject, Jessica corrected mentally.

"We can learn so much by studying the people who've lived before us," Ms. Shepard continued. "Past life-styles and customs can really give us insight into an era. For the next few weeks we'll be learning about the pioneers who settled in California during the 1840s."

Jessica groaned, along with the other kids in the class.

"Are we being punished or something?" Lila whispered. "Who cares about the stupid pioneers?"

"Teachers," Ellen Riteman, another Unicorn, whispered back.

"Quiet!" Mrs. Arnette commanded from the back.

Ms. Shepard waited until the noise died down. "I'm glad to see you're familiar with the subject," she said with a wry smile. "But perhaps you aren't familiar with the way I'm going to teach it. First of all, we won't be using any textbooks. Nothing I teach you about pioneers will come out of a book." She opened up a folder, pulled out a photograph, and began to walk up and down the aisles with it. "I think the best way for you to learn is for me to *show* you pioneer life, not tell you about. it."

Jessica leaned forward and stared curiously at the picture. It looked very old. It was about the size of a sheet of notebook paper and was a dull brownish color. Five people were in the photograph—a man, a woman, and three small children. They all wore dark, uncomfortable-looking clothing.

"As you've probably guessed, this is a re-production of a photograph of a pioneer family," Ms. Shepard explained. "Life back in the 1840s was very hard. Putting three meals on the table every day took an enormous amount of work. There were no microwaves, dishwashers, supermarkets, or refrigerators."

Ms. Shepard pointed to the grim-faced woman in the picture. "This pioneer woman was both a wife and a mother. Can any of you guess her age?"

All around the room, hands went up. Jessica was pleased when Ms. Shepard picked her.

"Well . . ." Jessica said, taking a moment to study the photograph. None of the woman's children looked older than four or five, but her face was lined and tired-looking. "She must be in her late twenties. How about twenty-eight?"

"Nice try," Ms. Shepard said, "but wrong. Actually, this pioneer mother was only nineteen."

"No way!" Jessica said.

Ms. Shepard nodded. "Pioneer women married young. This girl probably married when she was fourteen or fifteen."

"Fourteen!" Jessica exclaimed. "But that's only two years older than I am!"

"Exactly. See what I mean about past lifestyles being fascinating?" Ms. Shepard asked, setting the picture down. "OK, I have one more pioneer artifact to show you today."

Lila suddenly raised her hand.

"Yes? Do you have a question?" Ms. Shepard asked her.

"No," Lila said. "I'm just volunteering to help you show the next item."

"Great! Come on up. But I should warn you that this one is a little unusual."

"I don't mind. I want to help," Lila assured her eagerly, hurrying to the front of the room. "My name is Lila Fowler," she said. Then she proudly faced the class, flashing Jessica a smug smile. Lila was always trying to outdo Jessica.

When Ms. Shepard took out a long wooden stick with a curved top from the side of the desk, everyone had a guess about what it might be.

"A fishing pole?" Aaron said.

"A broken fishing pole," Winston Egbert joked.

"Part of a clothesline?" Elizabeth suggested.

"It looks like a giant question mark," Maria Slater said.

"Something you use to get groceries off a high shelf?" Jessica asked.

Ms. Shepard shook her head. "It's a shepherd's crook."

"Like in Little Bo-Peep?" Amy asked.

"Exactly," she answered. "Lila, step back a few feet and I'll show you how it works," Ms. Shepard said. She lightly hooked the curved part of the stick around Lila's ankle and tugged.

"Yeow!" Lila cried, almost losing her balance. The class erupted in laughter.

"See how it works?" the teacher said. "If a sheep starts to wander off, its owner pulls it back by tugging on its leg."

"Lila's a sheep!" Winston shouted. "Baa! Baa!"

Lila marched back to her seat, her face red.

Jessica snickered to herself. Social studies was fun after all!

Two

◇

"I'm going to get a banana split," Jessica decided, placing her menu down on the table at Casey's Place, where several of the Unicorns were gathered on Wednesday afternoon.

"I think I'll go for a butterscotch sundae," Lila said, "with extra whipped cream and cherries."

"Sounds good," Mandy Miller said.

"I'll have a banana split, too," said Janet Howell, an eighth-grader and the president of the Unicorn Club. "It might make me feel better."

"What's wrong, Janet?" Lila asked.

"I have a bad case of biology blues," she said with a sigh.

"I know what you mean," Mary Wallace said sympathetically. "I'll probably have to stay up until midnight to get all my homework done."

"Teachers are inhuman," Janet said.

"Not all treachers," Mandy remarked. "Ms. Shepard's great."

"Who's Ms. Shepard?" Janet asked.

"I can't believe you haven't heard about her," Jessica said. "Everybody at school is talking about her. She's a student-teacher in our social studies class. She's young, and really pretty. Her class is awesome."

"She showed us how to use berries and plants for makeup," Ellen Riteman added, sipping her ice water.

"A teacher talked about makeup?" Janet asked, beginning to look interested. "During class?"

"Yep," Lila answered. "She even let me try some on. I looked great."

"Today we panned for gold," Mandy said.

"Ms. Shepard brought in a big metal tub,"

Jessica explained, "and filled it with dirt and water, and then sprinkled gold pieces in it."

"Not real gold pieces," Ellen interrupted. "Fool's gold."

"But it looked like real gold," Jessica said.

Janet rolled her eyes. "This is embarrassing. We're sitting here talking about school." She glanced around the restaurant. "I hope nobody overheard us."

"All right, here's a more exciting subject," Lila said. "My father's buying a new sports car. We went to the Jaguar dealership yesterday, and I talked him into getting a blazing red one."

Uh-oh, Jessica thought. *This sounds like the beginning of another Unicorn bragging session.*

"I've got even more exciting news than that," Janet said. "My parents rented a house in Lake Tahoe. It's right on the ski slopes."

"My parents said I could redecorate my room," Ellen said. "New carpeting, new curtains, new wallpaper, and a four-poster bed. It's going to be gorgeous!"

Jessica sighed. She tried to think of something exciting going on in her life, something that would make them sit up and take notice.

"Guess what?" she said, trying to make her voice sound bright. "I just got a video of 'Testify.' "

Lila gave Jessica a patronizing smile. "Coco's video is awesome, isn't it? But watching it on your family's old TV is a waste. It's practically prehistoric—the sound isn't even in stereo."

It's not fair! Jessica thought, fuming. *Why don't I have anything to brag about?* It was true that a while back her aunt Helen had given her a hundred dollars as a gift, but Jessica didn't even have anything to show for it. Instead of spending the money on herself, she had spent it on her friends.

If only I had been born rich . . . Jessica thought miserably.

"Hey, you don't need to slam the door," Steven Wakefield complained as Jessica burst into the house late on Friday afternoon.

Jessica made a face at her brother. As usual, he was on the phone talking to his girlfriend, Cathy Connors. "Don't start with me, Steven," Jessica warned.

"Then make like Houdini and disappear," he retorted.

"Steven, if only I could trade you in for a red Jaguar or a trip to Lake Tahoe," she muttered, and left the room.

Jessica went upstairs, slammed her bedroom door behind her, and flung herself on her bed. She couldn't believe how unfair life was sometimes.

Elizabeth came through the bathroom that connected the twins' bedrooms and poked her head into Jessica's room. "It's your turn to set the table tonight," Elizabeth reminded her sister.

Jessica rolled over and moaned. "Of course it is. My whole life is a complete disaster."

"What's wrong?" Elizabeth asked.

"You wouldn't understand. But if you want to make me feel better, you could set the table for me. I don't even feel up to eating dinner tonight."

"Really?" Elizabeth said with a sly smile. "Mom's surprise probably isn't all that big a deal, anyway."

"Surprise?" Jessica asked, raising one eyebrow. "What is it?"

"I don't know. I think it's pretty big, because this morning when I asked Mom if I could have dinner over at Amy's, she acted really mysterious and said I couldn't. She wants the whole family to be there when she tells us."

Jessica's mind raced with exciting possibilities: a family trip to Europe, a winning lottery ticket, a new car. She jumped out of bed. "You know, Lizzie, I suddenly feel much better."

"The table looks lovely," Mrs. Wakefield commented as the family sat down for dinner. "Cloth napkins, the good china, and flowers. What a nice surprise, Jessica."

"Speaking of surprises," Jessica said, "Elizabeth told me you have one for us."

Mrs. Wakefield laughed. "So that explains the first-class treatment."

"What is it, Mom?" Steven asked. "Did you get one of those great chocolate cakes for dessert?"

Jessica rolled her eyes. Steven was always thinking of food.

Mrs. Wakefield smiled. "Well, I was going to wait until after dinner, but I get the distinct feeling my family couldn't hold out that long."

Jessica, Elizabeth, and Steven all nodded.

"I have some great news," Mrs. Wakefield began. "We've gotten an important new contract at work—a complete interior-design job for a four-story office building. That means a big bonus for me."

"How big?" Steven asked.

"Big enough to buy something really special for the four people I love the most—my family."

Jessica couldn't believe her ears. This was exactly what she had been dreaming about! *Just wait until Lila boasts about her father's stupid Jaguar again*, she thought. "What are we getting?" she asked.

"That's for all of us to decide together," her mother answered.

"Any suggestions?" Mr. Wakefield asked.

"I have hundreds of them!" Jessica exclaimed. "First I'll need a whole new wardrobe, then my own CD player, my own telephone—"

"What about me?" Steven interrupted. "High school's really tough, and I could use a vacation. How about sending me to Hawaii?"

"The point is to get something that the entire family can benefit from," Mrs. Wakefield reminded them.

Jessica's spirits sank. A *family* purchase. "You mean something boring, like a couch or a vacuum cleaner?"

"Not even close," her mother replied with a laugh. "Something we can all use, but something fun."

Just then a wonderful idea popped into Jessica's head. "I know the perfect thing!" she exclaimed. "It's something we really need, and it's for the whole family."

"What?" Mr. Wakefield asked.

"A big-screen TV!"

"Hey, great idea," Steven said.

"It's certainly a possibility. Elizabeth, what do you think?" Mrs. Wakefield asked.

"Lizzie wants a big-screen TV, too," Jessica cut in.

Elizabeth shook her head. "I think we should get a computer."

"A computer?" Steven repeated. "Hey, that's even better than a TV. We could get all sorts of cool games."

"That's a good idea, honey," Mrs. Wakefield said. "It would be fun *and* educational."

Jessica stared at her family in horror. She couldn't believe they were serious. *How can I be related to such boring people?* she wondered. "But a big-screen TV would be much more fun," she argued. "Our TV is ancient, and the screen is so tiny. The sound isn't even stereo," she added, remembering what Lila had said.

"We have a perfectly good TV," Mr. Wakefield said calmly. "We don't have a computer."

"We don't *need* a computer," Jessica argued. "Everyone knows that only nerds use computers."

"A computer would be great!" Elizabeth said. "I can do the *Sixers* layout and all my reports for school on it."

"Mom hasn't made her decision yet," Jessica snapped.

"Well, let's vote on it now," Mrs. Wakefield suggested. "All in favor of a new TV, raise your hand."

Jessica raised her hand high, but she was the only one.

Four hands went up in favor of the computer.

"You've been outvoted," Steven told her.

"It's not fair!" Jessica wailed, standing up

and glaring at her twin. "This is all your fault, Elizabeth. Everybody was happy with my big-screen TV idea until you brought up the computer."

"You'll love having a computer in the house, Jess," Elizabeth said.

"It'll be horrible," Jessica said angrily, and stormed out of the room.

Three

◇

"What a waste of a Saturday afternoon," Jessica grumbled as she climbed into her family's car.

"I thought you loved going to the mall, Jess," Elizabeth said, squeezing into the backseat next to her.

"We're not going to the mall for normal stuff," Jessica complained. "We're going for a stupid computer. Why are Mom and Dad making me come along, anyway? If any of my friends see me, my reputation will be ruined. They'll all think I'm a computer nerd."

"You're exaggerating, Jess."

"I might as well start wearing my glasses

all the time and get one of those pocket protectors. I'll never be popular again."

Elizabeth laughed.

"I knew you wouldn't understand," Jessica said, and turned her face to the window.

Minutes later, Jessica was reluctantly following her family into the computer store. *What a major bore*, she thought. Everywhere she looked she saw computers, more computers, and computer supplies. To her left were boxes of computer paper; to her right was a display of plastic boxes with slots in the front. She couldn't figure out why they cost hundreds of dollars.

She bent over a display case with a wide selection of games: Invisible Invaders, Vanishing Shadows, Phreaky Phantoms. *Kid stuff*, she thought dismissively.

As she passed the cash register, though, a large white sign caught her attention: Free With Purchase of Complete Computer System—Portable Stereo Cassette/CD Player.

A portable CD player—now that's interesting, Jessica thought. She walked over to the display and inspected the sample boom box, which was tuned to one of the local rock stations. It was compact enough to be portable, but it sounded great. Suddenly getting a computer didn't sound like such a bad idea to Jessica.

She hurried over to her family and tapped Elizabeth on the shoulder. "So, how's it going?"

Elizabeth turned around, a look of surprise on her face. "OK, but what do you care? I thought you didn't want anything to do with this."

"It's just that I don't understand them . . . all those cables and disk thingies." She pointed at the computer Elizabeth was looking at. "Is this the one we're getting?"

"Maybe," Elizabeth replied. "It has a great display, and it's really fast. Why the sudden interest, Jessica?"

"I can change my mind, can't I?" Jessica said, imagining the look on Lila's face when she saw the boom box. Lila had an impressive stereo system in her room, but she didn't have a sleek-looking portable one that she could bring to the beach and Unicorn meetings.

Elizabeth looked suspiciously at her sister.

"And it just so happens there's a free gift

with the purchase of a computer system," Jessica admitted. "It's a really cool-looking boom box."

"Aha!" Elizabeth exclaimed. "I knew there had to be something behind this."

"All right, I admit it. The box will be great for the beach, won't it?"

"It does sound perfect."

"I may even let you borrow it," Jessica said.

"What makes you think Mom and Dad will give it to *you*?" Elizabeth demanded.

"Well, since you're getting your dumb computer, I deserve the box. It's only fair."

"The box should be for the whole family, too, not just for you," Elizabeth argued.

"We'll see what Mom and Dad say," Jessica said, confident that her parents would see things her way.

But Jessica was wrong. On the drive home, her parents told her firmly that the boom box, like the computer, was a family purchase.

"You'll get a turn to use it," Mrs. Wakefield told her. "But it will belong to all of us."

"Have I got a surprise for you!" Ms. Shepard said in social studies class Tuesday morning. "We're going on a three-day field trip this Friday, Saturday, and Sunday!"

An excited buzz circled the classroom, and Ms. Shepard held up her hand for quiet. "Since we're studying pioneers, we're going to experience pioneer life firsthand. There's an authentic, working pioneer farm over in Corona Valley. It's owned jointly by the state historical society and Sweet Valley College, and every semester a few college students like me live there to help run the farm and guide school groups who come to visit. All of Mrs. Arnette's classes are going to get to spend a weekend there, and you're the first!"

Excited chatter filled the room.

"Is that where you got all the neat pioneer stuff?" Maria Slater asked, and Ms. Shepard nodded.

"Are there cows and horses there?" Aaron Dallas asked.

"Yep. The pioneer farm is run just like it would have been in the middle of the last century. So there aren't any tractors—we use horses to pull the plows. The caretakers and college students do all the chores. We work as the pioneers did: raising crops, milking cows, baking bread, pumping water, chopping wood, and lots more. It's wonderful."

In the back of the room, Mrs. Arnette stood up and began handing out information sheets and permission forms. "It's a worthwhile experience. I'll be chaperoning the girls and Coach Cassels will be chaperoning the boys. For three days we'll live like the pioneers did one hundred and fifty years ago."

Jessica grinned at Lila. "Can you believe this? Three days in the country! It's going to be great!"

Lila shrugged. "Working on a farm doesn't sound so great to me."

Jessica grinned. "Oh, I'm not worried about that. You know what's really going to be great?"

Lila shook her head.

"No school on Friday!"

Four

◇

"Do you know what this permission slip says?" Maria Slater said later that day at lunch. She wore an expression of comic horror on her face.

Elizabeth laughed. Maria was an actress and had appeared in many films and television commercials when she was younger. She could be very dramatic when she wanted to.

"No, I haven't looked at it," Elizabeth said. "Doesn't it just say the usual? 'I, blank, give permission for my child, blank, to go to blank'?"

"Well," Maria said, "I think you should read it."

Amy Sutton pulled a crumpled piece of paper out of her backpack and smoothed it out.

Her eyes widened as she read. "Wow! Look at all the stuff we're not allowed to take to the pioneer farm!"

Brooke Dennis peered over Amy's shoulder. "Blow dryers, radios, junk food, curling irons, makeup . . . aren't we allowed to bring *anything*?"

"I guess the point is that since we're going to an old-fashioned place, we can't bring anything modern," Maria said.

"Ms. Shepard wasn't kidding when she said we'd be living like pioneers," Elizabeth added.

"You mean cave dwellers," Amy joked.

"It'll be an adventure, that's for sure," Maria said.

"Hey," Amy said, pointing across the cafeteria to the Unicorner, the table where the Unicorns always sat. "I wonder if the Snob Squad have read their permission slips yet."

"I bet they haven't," Brooke said with a grin. "They look too happy."

"They won't be for long," Maria observed wryly. "The Unicorns can't exist without makeup and hair dryers and nail polish."

"Poor Jessica," Elizabeth mused. "She's not

going to like this at all. She uses almost every one of the items on that list every morning! Maybe I should go over there and warn her."

"Oh, let me, Elizabeth," Amy begged with a mischievous gleam in her eyes.

"OK, but let the Unicorns down easy," Elizabeth said, laughing.

"I'll try, but you know them," Amy said, getting up and heading toward the Unicorner. "Prepare for some fireworks!"

"You have *got* to be joking," Ellen Riteman said.

"OK, but don't say I didn't warn you." Amy shrugged and headed back to her friends' table.

Jessica quickly dug out her permission slip and read it. "Amy's right," Jessica said, horrified. "No blow dryers, radios, makeup—there's about a zillion absolutely necessary things we can't bring!"

Ellen slumped in her chair. "No makeup?" she whined. "I don't want anyone to see me without makeup. Especially boys!"

"Ms. Shepard can't be serious," Lila complained. "Three whole days without any of this stuff? No way!"

"I don't have an appetite anymore," Jessica grumbled, pushing away her sandwich.

Janet Howell smiled sweetly. "Three days of pioneer horror for you poor sixth-graders. I'm glad I'm in eighth grade."

"Oh, I don't know," Mary Wallace said. "The trip sounds like fun, and I bet after a day you won't even miss the things you can't bring. I wish seventh-graders were invited—I'd love to stay at a pioneer farm."

"You'd want to go?" Lila asked, surprised.

"Sure. It's only three days, after all," Mary said.

Jessica looked at the list again. The trip *was* only three days, and the whole adventure of living on a pioneer farm did sound pretty fun. Still, no makeup? None?

"I don't believe Ms. Shepard really expects us to live like this," Lila said, a thoughtful expression on her face. "This list has to be an exaggeration."

"I bet you're right, Lila," Ellen said. "She's probably just trying to get us used to the idea that it won't be a very modern place. Like there's probably not a really good stereo or TV there, and the bathrooms probably have only one electrical outlet."

"Are you sure the farm has *any* electricity?" Mary asked. "The pioneers survived without it."

"Of course there's electricity," Jessica scoffed. "There has to be some electricity for lights and air conditioning, and stuff."

"You'd better hope you're right, Jessica," Janet said. "If there isn't any electricity, then you guys are going to miss the Aid the People concert this weekend." The concert was a benefit for victims of a typhoon in southern Asia. It was being held in San Francisco and was going to be broadcast live on TV and radio stations.

"*Oh, no!*" Lila cried. "*This weekend?* I totally forgot about it! I can't go on this dumb trip— my father got me tickets to see it live!"

"Mrs. Arnette did say that anyone who didn't want to go could do a twenty-five-page report on pioneer life-styles instead," Mandy Miller pointed out.

"*Twenty-five pages?*" Lila repeated.

"Oh, come on, Lila," Jessica said. "Come

to the pioneer farm. You can watch the concert on TV with the rest of us."

"I hope for your sakes that there's a TV or at least a stereo there," Janet said with a smirk.

"There's got to be a TV," Jessica said. "Maybe it's only black-and-white, though," she added sadly.

"Now that's what I call primitive," Lila put in.

"Well, any TV will do," Ellen said. "Pioneers can't be picky."

Jessica sighed. "It's better than nothing."

"If you guys are so worried about it, why don't you just ask Ms. Shepard?" Mary suggested. "I'm sure she's around here somewhere."

"Good idea, Mary," Lila said, jumping up. "Come on, Jessica. Let's go."

The two girls made their way through the crowded cafeteria and found Ms. Shepard at a table with some other teachers.

"Hi, girls," Ms. Shepard said. "What's up?"

"Um . . . we were wondering," Jessica began, "if—well, the Aid the People concert is going to be on TV and on the radio this weekend, and we wanted to make sure the pioneer farm has a decent TV or stereo or something."

Ms. Shepard smiled. "I'm sorry, girls, but everything on the farm is just as it was a hundred and fifty years ago. There's no TV."

"Is there a stereo?" Jessica whispered, a sinking feeling in her stomach.

"Nope. There's no electricity at all. That's why we told you not to bring electrical appliances—there's no place to plug them in."

"Thank you," Jessica said glumly, and she and Lila slowly walked back to their table. This weekend didn't sound like any fun at all!

Elizabeth and her friends were leaving the lunchroom when they heard voices behind them.

"Elizabeth! Wait up!"

Elizabeth turned around and saw Todd Wilkins hurrying to catch up with her. Aaron Dallas, Ken Matthews, Randy Mason, and Charlie Cashman were with him.

"What's going on?" Elizabeth asked.

"We were looking at the permission slips for the pioneer-farm trip during lunch," Ken explained, "and we were trying to figure out whether we'd be allowed to bring baseball equipment. But we couldn't decide whether that was too modern. Todd thought you might know whether baseball had been invented by the 1840s."

"Hmm," Elizabeth said. "I'm not sure. I think it might have been invented a little later than that, though."

"That's what I thought, too," Randy agreed. "I guess that means we can't bring our mitts and stuff."

"That's too bad," Maria said. "I love baseball."

"You play baseball?" Randy asked, looking surprised.

"Sure," Maria responded.

"Oh, come on," Aaron said with a smirk. "Girls can't play baseball."

"What are you talking about?" Maria demanded. "Of course we can."

"Baseball's not only for boys, you know," Brooke put in. "I don't get a chance to play all that often, but I watch all of the Dodgers' games on TV."

"I bet you polish your nails all the way

through the game," Charlie Cashman sneered. "Gee, what was that? A home run touchdown?" he mocked in falsetto.

Elizabeth began to get annoyed. "Charlie, cut it out. We all know how to play baseball. Belinda Layton is better than any of you guys."

"Nah, all most girls know how to do is put on makeup," Charlie retorted. "Hey, come to think of it, you're gonna have a pretty tough time at the pioneer farm. Eek! No hair dryers allowed!" he said.

"Shut up, Charlie," Amy warned.

Randy laughed. "Well, you've got to admit, the girls are going to have a hard time getting along without makeup and curling irons and all that stuff. Pioneer life's a lot easier on us boys. We're tougher."

Elizabeth was surprised to hear Randy talking like that. He was one of the smartest boys in the sixth grade, and she hadn't thought he would believe stereotypes about girls. "What do you mean, you're tougher?" Elizabeth asked. "That's just not true. Boys aren't any tougher than girls. And pioneer women worked hard, you know."

"They did all the housework," Aaron said. "How hard can that be?"

"It's plenty hard," Elizabeth argued. "You try carrying heavy pails full of water a half a mile from the river. And women didn't just do housework, either. Women cleared land and farmed and chopped wood, too. Right, Todd?"

Charlie spoke up before Todd had a chance to open his mouth. "Pioneer women didn't do any of that stuff. Girls back then were just as weak as they are now. Right, Todd?"

Todd looked uncomfortable. "Well," he began slowly, "I don't think girls are as strong as boys are—"

"See?" Charlie cut in, looking at Elizabeth. "Todd agrees that girls are nothing but a bunch of wimps."

"How could you say that, Todd?" Elizabeth demanded, turning away from Aaron to glare at Todd.

"I didn't mean—" Todd began.

"You guys are unbelievable!" Amy shouted. "Just you wait and see. Girls can handle pioneer life a whole lot better than boys!"

Just then Jessica wandered over on her way

to her locker. "Hi, everyone. What's going on, Elizabeth?"

"The boys say girls aren't as tough as boys and can't handle pioneer life," Elizabeth reported.

"Well, that's stupid," Jessica said simply.

"No it's not," Ken said, "and I can prove it. Jessica, do you or do you not use makeup, a hair dryer, a curling iron, and all that junk every morning?"

"Sure I do," Jessica replied.

"See? Girls are held together with makeup and hair goop. You're not going to have any of those things at the farm. I guarantee you're going to fall apart on the first day."

Elizabeth glanced at her twin and saw a spark in Jessica's blue-green eyes. "I know who's going to do the falling apart, and it's not going to be the girls," Jessica snapped back. "Which one of you is going to be able to go for half an hour without a Coke or nachos or a candy bar? You're not allowed to bring junk food, either, you know."

"No problem," Ken bragged. "Hey, I can eat raw wheat right off the stalk if I have to.

Todd and Charlie are right—it's the girls who won't be able to handle pioneer life."

"Oh, yeah?" Elizabeth countered. "Well, just wait until this weekend. We'll see who can really live like pioneers," she said, throwing Todd an angry look.

"Wanna bet?" Todd said.

Elizabeth didn't hesitate for a second. She looked at her sister and her friends, and turned to Todd with a sweet smile. "You're on, Wilkins!"

Five

That night Elizabeth sat at the family's new computer. "OK, that should be it," she said, leaning back to review her work on the screen. After she checked for errors, she tapped a couple of keys and the printer began whirring smoothly. A minute later she held a neatly printed sheet of paper in her hand.

"It's finished," she announced, walking into Jessica's room.

Jessica, stretched out on the bed, looked up from the latest issue of *Image*. "What's finished?"

"Well, if we're going to have a bet with the boys about who can handle pioneer life better, we have to have some way to decide who wins," Elizabeth explained.

"You mean we have to have some way to show the boys that we've won," Jessica said with a grin. "I can't believe how annoying they are."

"I know. And I can't believe Todd went along with them," Elizabeth said, sighing.

"Don't worry, Lizzie," Jessica said comfortingly. "We'll make them change their minds about girls."

Elizabeth nodded. "Anyway, I went back over the list of the things we can't bring with us to the pioneer farm, and I made up a sort of contract. Todd said he was going to get all the boys in our social studies class to agree to the bet, and I told him I'd get all the rest of the girls in the class to agree to it, so I think everyone in the class should sign the contract."

"That makes sense," Jessica said, reaching for the piece of paper Elizabeth was holding. "Hey, this looks really professional. How did you manage to get the word *agreement* in such big letters?"

"I did it on the computer," Elizabeth answered.

"Oh," Jessica said, continuing to read. "What's this stuff about a speech?"

Elizabeth grinned. "It's my stroke of genius. We can't have a bet without some kind of payoff, right? When the girls win the bet, Todd has to make a speech in the cafeteria on Monday afternoon about why girls are better than boys."

Jessica laughed. "Oh, I love it! Just one thing, though—I think he should have to talk for at least ten minutes. We don't want to let him off too easily."

"OK," Elizabeth agreed. "I'll go back to the computer and add it."

Suddenly Jessica looked thoughtful. "Hey, what if the boys win?"

"Then I'll make a speech on why boys are better than girls. But don't worry—I'm sure we'll win. Can you imagine Charlie Cashman giving up junk food for three whole days, or Todd not being able to practice his slam dunk?"

"Or Aaron not having perfectly blow-dried hair?" Jessica added, giggling.

"This bet is going to be fun," Jessica continued. "But it's too bad I can't take my new boom box with me."

"*Our* new boom box," Elizabeth corrected. "Even if we hadn't made the bet, though, you still couldn't have taken it. It's a modern electrical device."

"It runs on batteries," Jessica reminded her. "Didn't they have batteries back then?"

Elizabeth rolled her eyes. "I don't think so. Anyway, even if they did, they certainly didn't have radios or CD players."

Jessica sighed. "I don't know why they couldn't have gotten around to inventing them back then. If they had, I wouldn't have to miss the Aid the People concert."

Elizabeth hid a smile. Only Jessica would want to change history so that she could catch a concert. "Mom could videotape it for you," she suggested.

"I know," Jessica said. "But it's not the same. And besides, they're going to give away two free tickets—plus backstage passes—to a concert of the winner's choice. Anyone who donated to the Aid the People fund is eligible. I called last week and pledged five dollars so I could have a chance at winning the tickets. I'd love to see Johnny Buck again."

"You're also helping the typhoon victims, Jess. That's really nice," Elizabeth said.

"I guess," Jessica said, not really listening. "But I wish we weren't going on the field trip *this* weekend."

"I got this fantastic new bathing suit," Janet told the rest of the Unicorns the next day at lunch. "The house we'll be staying at in Lake Tahoe has this unbelievable hot tub."

"What color is the suit?" Lila asked before biting into a pear.

"Lavender with yellow and purple flowers."

"That'll look good on you," Lila commented.

"I think I'm going to get lavender wallpaper for my room," Ellen said.

Jessica was getting tired of listening to her friends talk about the trips they were taking and the new things they were getting. Of course, if Jessica had had something more interesting than part ownership in a boom box to talk about, she would have been doing the same thing.

Jessica had turned her attention to eating her chicken-salad sandwich when she heard a familiar voice behind her.

"Hey, Jessica."

Jessica's heart beat a little faster. It was Aaron Dallas! She really liked Aaron, and he was standing with Jake Hamilton, a really cute seventh-grader.

"Hi, Aaron. Hi, Jake," she said. "What's up?"

"Elizabeth just told me you got a new computer," Aaron said.

Oh, great, Jessica thought miserably. *Thanks to my big-mouth sister, everyone, including Aaron, will think I'm some kind of nerd.*

"That's right," she said slowly. "So?"

"Well, there are a couple of programs Jake and I really want to try out," Aaron replied. "I'd love to come over sometime and use your computer for a little while."

Jessica's mouth nearly dropped open. "You would?"

"If it's all right with you," Aaron said.

A smile spread across her face. "Sure. Anytime," she said.

"Is this afternoon OK? Maybe about four o'clock?"

Jessica nodded, feeling almost dizzy with

sudden happiness. *Maybe this computer isn't such a drag after all.*

"See you then," Aaron said. He and Jake waved to the other Unicorns and walked off.

"I can't believe that Aaron and Jake are coming over to your house—this afternoon!" Lila cried. "I didn't know they liked computers! You know, Jessica," Lila continued, "I would be interested in seeing it, too."

"You can come over sometime, if you want."

"I might have some time today," Lila said innocently.

"OK," Jessica said. She knew perfectly well that Lila was less interested in the computer than in the boys who wanted to use it.

"Can I come, too?" Ellen asked.

"And me?" Janet added. "I think it would be, uh, useful to know something about computers."

Within a few minutes, all the Unicorns had made plans to meet at Jessica's house at four o'clock that afternoon.

Jessica smiled to herself. If she had known how impressed everyone would be with her family's computer, she would have bragged about it sooner!

"I'm really looking forward to seeing your computer," Amy said as she watched Elizabeth open her locker.

"You and the rest of the *Sixers* staff," Elizabeth said with a laugh. "Nora, Julie, Maria, and a few others will be there, too."

"Where's your sister?" Amy asked. "I thought she was going to walk home with us today."

Elizabeth shrugged. "The Unicorns are probably having an emergency meeting because Janet ran out of mascara," she joked.

"Maybe they're taking a vote on what kind of new hairstyle Ellen should have," Amy said with a laugh.

"In that case, we won't see Jessica for hours!"

"Oh, Aaron, you know *so* much about computers," Jessica said as she led a group of her friends into the Wakefield house.

"Well, I hack around a little at school," Aaron replied modestly. "They have IBMs. What kind is yours, Jessica?"

Jessica shrugged. "It's cream-colored with a tan thing on the front," she said. "Come on in and see for yourself."

With her friends following, Jessica headed for the den. The moment she entered the room, however, she stopped short. The den was crowded with members of the *Sixers* staff!

Jessica marched over to Elizabeth and put her hands on her hips. "Clear out," she ordered. "We need to use the computer."

"Since when do you even know how to turn it on?" Elizabeth said, glancing over at the group of kids standing at the doorway. "What are you all doing here?"

"Aaron and Jake want to use it, and everyone else wants to see how it works," Jessica said.

Lila came over to where the twins were standing. "What's the problem, Jessica? Why are all these people here?"

"We're working on the school newspaper," Elizabeth answered. "We'll probably be finished in an hour or so."

"An hour! We don't want to wait that long," Jessica told her sister.

"Well, sorry. We're not done yet," Elizabeth said, turning back to the computer.

Jessica glared at her. "Elizabeth, I can't believe you're being so selfish. This was a family purchase, remember? The last time I checked, I was still part of the family."

Elizabeth turned around again. "Jess, you don't even know how to use it."

"Aaron is a computer expert," Jessica said, her voice rising. "He can show me."

"Nobody's showing you anything now," Elizabeth said, her tone matching Jessica's. "We're not going anywhere!"

"Yes you are!" Jessica insisted loudly. She went around behind the computer and grabbed the cord, intending to pull it out of the wall socket.

"*Jessica! Don't you dare!*" Elizabeth shouted.

"It's my computer, too! I'll do what I want with it!"

"Jessica! Elizabeth! What's all the commotion about?" Mrs. Wakefield made her way through the crowd of kids in the Wakefields' den and came to a stop in front of the twins.

"She started it!" both girls said at the same time, each pointing to the other.

"Mom, we were using the computer first, for *Sixers* business," Elizabeth explained. "Then

Jessica marched in here and wanted us to get off right away. She almost pulled the plug out of the wall!"

"It's my turn. I've never gotten a chance to use it!" Jessica cried.

Mrs. Wakefield shook her head. "No one's going to use it if you're going to behave like two-year-olds." To Jessica's mortification, her mother turned to the other kids. "I'm sorry, but we're going to turn off the computer now. I'm sure Jessica and Elizabeth will arrange for you to use it another day."

Jessica and Elizabeth apologized to their friends and sent them out the door.

"Girls, I'm sorry to see you behaving this way to each other," Mrs. Wakefield said.

"It's Elizabeth's fault," Jessica said, pouting.

Mrs. Wakefield sighed. "You both have to remember that sharing is an important part of being a family—and of being friends. Long after this computer is on the junk heap, you two will still be sisters."

"You're right," Elizabeth said sincerely.

Jessica didn't say anything. She was still furious at her sister and humiliated at having been yelled at in front of her friends.

After Mrs. Wakefield had left the room, Jessica turned to Elizabeth. "I can't believe you did that in front of my friends," she whispered.

"I can't believe *you*," Elizabeth whispered back. "I wasn't the one who started the fight!"

"You did so," Jessica said stubbornly.

"I did not!" Elizabeth cried.

World War Wakefield had begun.

Six

◇

"What do you think of this belt?" Jessica asked Lila on Thursday afternoon at the Valley Mall. The girls were shopping for clothing to wear on their field trip.

"Not pioneer-looking enough," Lila said.

"I don't know about this," Jessica complained as she put back the belt. "This pioneer thing isn't exactly my style."

"Mine either," Lila replied, "but since we're going to have to do without all the essentials this weekend, we might as well have the right clothes."

"I think this one's pretty—and kind of pioneerish," Jessica said, holding up a red leather belt decorated with evenly spaced silver medallions.

Lila's eyes narrowed. "Hmm . . . no, too sophisticated. Try this one," she said, tossing a simple tawny leather one over to Jessica.

"I think it's too plain," Jessica commented.

"No, it's just right," Lila said. "Very, uh, farmlike."

Jessica shrugged and glanced at the price tag. *For a plain strip of leather, it's awfully expensive,* she thought.

Just then she caught sight of Lila, wallet in hand, heading over to the cash register with the red-and-silver belt.

"Hey!" Jessica called, putting down the plain belt and hurrying over to her. "I saw that belt first. You said it was too sophisticated!"

"For you, I meant," Lila said casually. "Not for me. Besides, you couldn't afford it."

Jessica knew Lila was right. Even so, she was irritated. It was just like Lila to get something *she* wanted and make a cutting remark at the same time.

All the way home from the mall Jessica seethed inside. Things were definitely not going her way lately. Lila had something else to show off, and thanks to Elizabeth, Jessica hadn't been able to impress Aaron, Jake, and the Unicorns with the new computer. Instead, she'd been embarrassed.

When she got home, Jessica began to pack for the next day's trip. She stuffed some jeans, shirts, underwear, and socks into her suitcase, and tossed her comb and brush on top. She went into the bathroom to collect her soap and shampoo. She let out a sigh when she looked at the drawer that contained all her makeup. As she marched out of the bathroom, her eyes fell on the boom box, which was sitting on top of her dresser.

Suddenly she had an idea. She remembered how worked up Elizabeth had gotten over the bet between the girls and the boys, and the speech that the loser would have to give in the cafeteria. Then Jessica thought about how much she wanted to hear the Aid the People concert and find out if she had won tickets to a Johnny Buck concert.

Jessica glanced again at the boom box on the dresser. With one simple act, she realized, she could get even with Elizabeth, listen to the concert, *and* have all her friends be unbelievably grateful to her!

"Single file, people," Coach Cassels ordered the sixth-graders as they boarded the school bus that would take them to the pioneer farm.

"No school today—all *right!*" Amy said to Elizabeth as they stood in line.

"I can't wait to see the farm," Elizabeth said. "I hope I get to ride the horses."

"Want to sit in the back?" Amy said as they climbed up the steps of the bus.

Elizabeth nodded and followed Amy to the rear. When Jessica climbed in a minute later, she didn't even say hello to Elizabeth.

"Is Jessica ignoring you or something?" Amy asked.

"She's still mad at me," Elizabeth said. "It's all because of the mix-up with the computer the other day."

Just then the engine roared and the bus shuddered into gear.

The forty-five-minute bus ride passed quickly as Elizabeth talked with Amy, Maria,

Melissa McCormick, and Julie Porter. A few times she glanced at Jessica and felt sad. She hated to fight with Jessica.

In no time the bus was turning onto a dirt road and winding through fields of tall corn and alfalfa plants.

"We're here!" Elizabeth said, peering past Amy's shoulder to look out the window. They drove by a peaked red barn, passed a couple of tall oak and maple trees, and came to a stop in front of a large farmhouse.

As Elizabeth stepped off the bus, she noticed two women greeting Ms. Shepard. They wore long gathered dresses and lace-up shoes. One had a white apron tied around her waist.

When all the students had gotten off the bus, Ms. Shepard introduced the two women as Ms. Emburg and Ms. Swaine, the pioneer farm's caretakers.

"College students like myself are here for only one semester, and school groups stay for the weekend, but Ms. Emburg and Ms. Swaine live here year-round," Ms. Shepard explained.

"Are the other college students here now?" Elizabeth asked.

"No," Ms. Shepard answered with a grin.

"They have the weekend off, and you will take their places running the farm."

"By ourselves?" Jessica asked.

Ms. Shepard nodded.

"But how will we know what to do?" Ellen Riteman added.

"One of the caretakers or teachers will show you the ropes," Mrs. Arnette put in. "We'll divide up the chores. Each of you will get a chance to participate in all aspects of farm life."

There were a couple of groans, and Ms. Shepard looked around, an expression of concern on her face. "Tell you what—let's split up into groups and take a tour of the farm. You'll see that although there is a lot of work to do here, you can have a lot of fun, too."

Elizabeth was put in Ms. Shepard's group with Amy, Julie, and Maria. Jessica and most of her Unicorn friends were assigned to Mrs. Arnette's group.

The first building Ms. Shepard took her group to was the main farmhouse. On the ground floor was a big kitchen with a wood-burning stove. Another room contained several large dining tables.

Next Ms. Shepard took them to the bunk-houses. "These aren't original," she explained, "though we modeled them after bunkhouses found on ranches throughout the West. We built them to accommodate the students who come here on weekends." One building was for the boys, she told them, the other was for the girls. Mrs. Arnette and Coach Cassels would stay in the main house with the caretakers and college students.

"It's exciting, isn't it?" Ms. Shepard said, smiling. "Everything's just as it was a hundred and fifty years ago."

"Does that mean there's no running water?" Amy asked.

Ms. Shepard nodded.

"Do we have to carry it from the river, like we read about?" Elizabeth wondered.

"No," Ms. Shepard replied. "The river that's nearby isn't safe to drink from anymore, so we dug a well. We'll pump water into buck-ets and carry them into the house."

The teacher led them out of the bunkhouse and back toward the main house. "All of you will get a turn at chopping wood, picking fruits and vegetables, cooking meals, washing dishes, milking cows and goats, gathering eggs, feeding the animals—"

"The horses, too?" Elizabeth asked hopefully.

"Yep, horses included. There are eight horses, who do the heavy work of plowing and hauling. Those of you with riding experience will be able to ride them when they're not working, and you can help groom them."

Elizabeth's heart leaped and she smiled. Farm life was going to be wonderful!

"You'll be cooking, cleaning, and cutting wood, among other things," Mrs. Arnette was saying to her group of sixth-graders as she led them around the farm. "From the minute you wake up until it gets dark, farm chores will keep you busy. Pioneer children were very hard workers."

"Didn't pioneer kids ever have fun?" Jessica asked. She was beginning to worry. So far Mrs. Arnette had talked only about work—and work was not exactly her idea of a good time.

"Of course they had fun," Mrs. Arnette

said. "But only after all their chores were done."

"I don't think we're *ever* going to get done with all those chores," Ellen Riteman whispered to Jessica.

"I know what you mean," Jessica whispered back.

"When we're done with our chores tomorrow night, can we go to a restaurant or someplace where there's a TV and watch the Aid the People concert?" Lila asked hopefully.

But Mrs. Arnette just laughed. "Now, Lila, do you think the pioneers could just go out to a restaurant or turn on the TV? No, we're going to stay here and tell stories by candlelight. Doesn't that sound like fun?"

Not my kind of fun! Lila thought miserably.

Seven

◇

"I wonder what pioneers eat for lunch," Elizabeth said to Amy as they walked into the large dining room.

"I think we can be pretty sure it's not TV dinners," Amy joked.

Elizabeth laughed. "I'm so hungry, I'd eat anything. After two hours of pumping water and lugging it around, I'm totally exhausted."

"I know what you mean," Amy replied. "Hey, look who cooked lunch today!" she said, pointing toward the large, open hearth.

There stood Aaron Dallas and Mandy Miller, both wearing aprons. Mandy had a smear of gravy on her face, and she looked like she was having fun. Aaron, on the other hand, was slumped against the wall, limply spooning mashed potatoes onto plates.

"Tired, Aaron?" Elizabeth asked as she approached them.

Aaron straightened up and plunked some mashed potatoes on Elizabeth's plate. "Me? Nah. This is easy!"

Mandy put several slices of meat on Elizabeth's plate. "Sure thing, Aaron," she said. She grinned at Elizabeth. "Earlier I heard him telling Todd that his feet hurt."

Elizabeth, Amy, and Mandy all laughed. Aaron just scowled.

When they had gotten their food, Amy pointed to a table at the far end of the room. "There's Maria, Julie, and Melissa. Let's go sit with them."

"Isn't this place great?" Julie asked as Elizabeth and Amy sat down.

"Right out of a Hollywood western," Elizabeth replied, pouring milk from a pitcher into her glass.

"I once had a small part in a western," Maria said. "I got to ride a horse and wear a really uncomfortable costume. The horse part was fun, but the clothes made me appreciate T-shirts and jeans. Corsets itch!"

"Corsets sound gross," Amy said, stabbing a few green beans with her fork.

"But horseback riding is wonderful," Elizabeth said. "I don't know if I'm going to have enough time after I finish my chores to go riding, but at least I'll meet the horses. After lunch today, I'm assigned to feed them."

"Me, too," Amy said. "What about you guys?"

"I get to scrub pots and pans," Maria said.

Julie frowned. "I've got milking duty. I don't know the first thing about cows. I mean, I could probably find the thing the milk comes out of, but then what?"

Melissa laughed. "It's called an udder, Julie. And don't worry. I was talking to Ginny Lu Culpepper this morning, and she told me she's assigned to milk the cows today, too. She was raised on a farm in Tennessee, so I'm sure she'll know what to do."

Elizabeth gazed across the room at Jessica eating lunch with Lila and Ellen. Jessica still hadn't said a word to her. "I wonder what chores the Unicorns will be doing?" Elizabeth said.

Amy laughed. "Any chore here will be more than the Unicorns can handle. Unless it's talking about boys or shopping."

"Jessica knows how to do kitchen work, but she doesn't get much practice," Elizabeth added. "Somehow I usually wind up doing most of her chores at home."

"Well, it's going to be fun watching them try to be pioneer farmers," Amy said with a grin.

"Who's going to have time to watch?" Elizabeth said, pushing away her empty plate and standing up. "Come on, Amy—we've got a date with a mountain of hay and a pitchfork!"

"*Aaaah! Amy!*" Elizabeth screamed as she teetered on the ladder that led to the hayloft. The heavy pitchfork she had been carrying slipped from her fingers. "Amy! Help!" Elizabeth cried as both she and the pitchfork landed with a thump on the barn's dirt floor.

Amy stopped shoveling grain and rushed

over. *"Elizabeth!* Are you OK? Did the pitchfork hit you?"

Elizabeth stood up slowly, rubbing her thigh. "No, it didn't. I'm fine. Only my pride is wounded," she added as she saw Todd, Charlie, and Ken racing into the barn.

"Is everything OK in here?" Todd asked.

"Elizabeth fell off a ladder," Amy replied.

"But I'm OK," Elizabeth assured them.

Ken shook his head in mock sorrow. "See what happens when girls try to do men's work?"

Amy's face darkened. "Don't you have chores of your own to do?"

"We're taking a break," Charlie answered with a grin. "We've already chopped piles and piles of wood. Looks like you weaklings could use our help," he said, glancing at the wheelbarrow Elizabeth had been filling with hay. "I think the horses could use a little more to eat than just half a wheelbarrowful of hay."

"For your information," Elizabeth retorted, "this is my *fourth* wheelbarrowful of hay."

"Yeah," Amy added. "We have only two more horses left to feed. You know what I think, Elizabeth? I think these guys are resting because they're too tired to go on. I think they're afraid we'll win the bet and make them look like wimps!"

"In your dreams," Ken said.

"Oh, yeah? Well, why don't we come outside and count exactly how much wood you've cut?" Amy said.

"Come on, guys," Charlie said to Todd and Ken. "I don't think we're appreciated here. And to think we only came over to see if everything was all right!"

As they wandered off, Elizabeth and Amy exchanged glances and started to laugh. "They really didn't want us to see how much wood they chopped, did they?" Elizabeth said at last.

But before Amy could answer, a high-pitched scream pierced the air.

"Jessica! Ellen! Quick! Help! Make that—that *thing* go away!"

Inside the hen house, Jessica and Ellen stopped their work. "That's Lila!" Ellen cried as both girls dashed out the door, leaving their half-filled baskets of eggs behind.

Outside, a huge, hissing white goose, its

wings spread, had Lila cornered against a wire fence.

"Help!" Lila screamed again, her voice filled with terror. "Do something!" The goose hissed again and arched its slender neck toward Lila. She shrank back as far as she could, clutching her basket of eggs to her chest.

"What does it want, Lila?" Jessica called out. "What did you do to it?"

Just then several other sixth-graders, including Elizabeth and Amy, arrived on the scene and clustered behind Jessica and Ellen.

"I didn't do anything to it," Lila answered, her voice shaking. "I was just collecting eggs when it went crazy and attacked me! It's insane!"

"Maybe you took one of the goose's eggs," Elizabeth said. "Maybe she just wants her egg back."

"Lila," Jessica called, "do you have any goose eggs in that basket?"

"How should I know? I just picked up whatever eggs I saw lying around. It's not like they were labeled or anything. *Aaaaaaaaah!*" Lila shrieked again as the goose flapped its wings and pointed its sharp beak directly at her knee.

"Somebody get Ms. Shepard. Hurry!" Jessica yelled.

Just then the goose took another step toward Lila. Lila flung her basket and started to run from the angry goose. Eggs splattered and rolled in all directions, and as she ran, Lila skidded on an egg and went flying into the mud.

"It's going to kill me!" Lila cried when she saw the goose coming toward her again.

But the goose walked right past Lila and headed toward a big white egg that had escaped being broken. With an indignant squawk, the goose nudged it with her beak and then settled comfortably on top of it.

"Elizabeth was right!" Jessica said. "She just wanted her egg!"

Lila looked up. Her jeans were muddy and her new red-and-silver belt was covered with eggy goo.

Jessica clutched her stomach with both hands and howled with laughter.

Lila got up and tried to brush herself off, but only succeeded in rubbing the egg and mud into her clothes. "I'll tell you one thing," she said, humiliated. "I'm never eating another egg as long as I live."

*   *   *

The sun was getting low in the western sky by the time Elizabeth finished feeding the last horse, a big but gentle chestnut gelding named Slug.

"I wish I could pack Slug in my suitcase and take him home with me," Elizabeth told Amy.

"You'd have to have a pretty big suitcase," Amy teased.

Elizabeth laughed and gave the horse a final pat on his nose. "Slug's such a sweet horse. I hope I can ride him sometime this weekend."

Amy surveyed the horse's stall. "Are we done yet?" she asked.

"I think so," Elizabeth said. "Want to go over and see how Julie and Ginny Lu are doing with the milking?"

"Sure."

The two girls strolled over to the smaller barn and found Julie and Ginny Lu. To Elizabeth's surprise, Julie was milking a goat, not a cow.

"I thought you were going to milk the cows," Amy said.

Both Ginny Lu and Julie looked up. Ginny Lu was holding the animal steady for Julie, who was sitting next to her on a stool. Julie's hands were moving in a smooth rhythm, squirting milk from the goat into a pail.

"We finished that," Julie said between squirts.

"Can I try?" Elizabeth asked.

"Sure," Julie said, getting up. "Ginny Lu's a real pro at this—she can teach you."

"Great," Elizabeth said, sitting down on the stool. "Now, what do I do?"

"Place your hands here," Ginny Lu explained, pointing to the goat's udder. "Then squeeze with your thumbs in a kind of a downward motion. It's easy."

A little hesitantly, Elizabeth reached out and placed her hands and fingers on the goat's udder. She looked up. "This feels kind of weird."

"OK, now squeeze," Ginny Lu instructed.

Feeling really awkward, Elizabeth squeezed tentatively, but stopped abruptly, afraid she was hurting the goat. She peered around at the goat, who didn't seem to mind being milked. Elizabeth went back to work, squeezing a little harder this time. But no milk came out.

"It's not working," Elizabeth said. "I must be doing something wrong."

"That's because you're a girl," came Charlie Cashman's voice from behind her.

Elizabeth turned around to see Charlie, Ken, Aaron, and Randy entering the barn. *Oh, no*, she groaned inwardly.

Charlie nudged Aaron. "Another example of girls being wimps."

Aaron chuckled. "Like Lila freaking out over a harmless little goose."

"I didn't see any of you offering to help her," Elizabeth countered.

"Yeah," Amy said. "You weren't scared of a harmless little goose, too, were you?"

"No way," Charlie replied. "We were just having a lot of fun watching Lila, that's all."

"Right," Aaron added. "And we're having a lot of fun watching you, Elizabeth. Having a little trouble there?"

"She's just learning how," Julie said, defending Elizabeth.

Elizabeth flashed Julie a grateful smile. "I've almost got it figured out," she said.

"That's right," Ginny Lu said, her brown eyes flashing. "I'd like to see any of *you* get the hang of this."

"Move over," Charlie ordered, coming over and kneeling down next to Elizabeth. "I'll show you how it's done."

Elizabeth ignored him. Concentrating, she continued moving her thumbs as Ginny Lu had taught her. Out came a steady squirt of milk—right into Charlie's face!

In the light of an oil lamp, Jessica sank down onto the lumpy, musty bunk and pulled off her dust-covered shoes. She bent down and rubbed her feet. "Ow! This is only our first day, and I'm already exhausted. There's no way I'll be able to get up at six-thirty tomorrow morning."

Lila nodded sleepily from her own cot. "Me neither. I'll probably have nightmares all night of huge, horrible geese." She shivered. "I wish we'd never come here. I wish I were on my way to San Francisco to see the Aid the People concert tomorrow. I'd be staying in a really nice hotel, with a big, soft bed and a huge bathtub—" She stopped when Ellen tossed her pillow at her.

"We all feel bad enough already, Lila!" she said.

In the next bed over, Caroline Pearce was almost in tears. "Look at the size of this blister!" she wailed. "No one told me I was going to have to chop wood all afternoon!"

"I miss light bulbs," Mandy said with a sigh.

Surveying the scene in front of her, Jessica smiled with satisfaction. *They're really miserable,* she thought, forgetting her own aches and pains. *I can't wait to see the looks on their faces when I bring out the boom box!*

"What are *you* so happy about?" Lila demanded, catching sight of the smile on Jessica's face.

Jessica sat up and reached for her suitcase. "Drum roll, please!" she announced, bringing out the boom box. "Look what I brought!"

There were three or four gasps. "Your boom box!" Lila said in a loud whisper.

"Don't let Ms. Shepard or Mrs. Arnette see it," Caroline warned.

"Hey, isn't that going to make us lose the bet with the boys?" Mandy said.

Jessica shrugged. "Who cares? It's a dumb bet."

Just then the door to the bunkhouse opened. In came Elizabeth, Amy, Ginny Lu, Julie, and Maria.

"What's going on?" Amy asked.

"Jessica brought a boom box!" Caroline exclaimed.

Jessica glared at Caroline. "Thanks a lot," she said. She could tell from the way Elizabeth's blue-green eyes clouded over that she was very angry.

"Come here a second," Elizabeth said, grabbing Jessica's arm and pulling her off the cot. "How could you, Jessica?" Elizabeth said angrily when the two girls had gotten to the far corner of the room. "You've lost the bet for us! And you're breaking Ms. Shepard's rules!"

Jessica winced a little, but she reminded herself about the incident with the computer.

"It's a dumb bet. Listening to the Aid the People concert tomorrow evening is far more important," Jessica said.

"Jessica, I can't believe you!" Elizabeth said, nearly shouting.

"It's a free country," Jessica replied smugly. "I'll do what I want."

Elizabeth glared at her sister, and then turned and stormed out of the bunkhouse.

"It's just a dumb bet," Jessica muttered, but she couldn't help feeling worried. She had never seen that look in Elizabeth's eyes before.

Eight

◇

Jessica walked back to her bunk thoughtfully. She felt bad that Elizabeth was mad at her. *Maybe I should just put the boom box back in my suitcase so Elizabeth can still win the bet*, she thought.

"Oh, Jessica, I am *so* glad you brought the box!" Lila exclaimed, rushing over to her. "Now we don't have to miss the Aid the People concert tomorrow night, and we don't have to sit around and stare at the ceiling tonight," Lila rattled on. "Which CDs did you bring?"

"One of Coco's . . . and Johnny Buck's latest one," Jessica said slowly.

"Let's listen to Coco first," Ellen shouted from her cot.

"No, I hear that all the time," Brooke Dennis objected. Coco was Brooke's mother, and to Jessica's envy Brooke was planning to go on tour with her over the summer.

"Let's listen to the radio for a while, and save the CDs for later on," Caroline suggested.

Amy stood up. "Nobody should listen to anything. We all signed that contract with the boys, didn't we? If we use the boom box, we're going to lose the bet."

"You heard Jessica," Lila said airily. "It was a dumb bet anyway."

"Besides, it's Elizabeth who'll have to give the speech, not any of us," Ellen said, brushing back her short brown hair. "She's good at that stuff. She won't mind."

Amy gave an exasperated sigh and flopped back down onto her cot.

As Jessica listened to the other girls all pleading with her to play the box, it was becoming harder and harder to resist. Jessica had something all her friends wanted, and they seemed like they would do almost anything if she would let them use it. She loved the feeling of power.

"You're going to let me listen to Johnny Buck because I'm your best friend, aren't you?" Lila asked.

"That all depends," Jessica said, her eyes sparkling.

"On what?" Lila said.

"On what you'll do for me. I'm assigned kitchen duty tomorrow, but I'm *sooo* tired . . ." Jessica stretched lazily on her cot.

Lila stood up angrily. "You want *me* to do your chores?"

Jessica suddenly realized that there were some things that even the lure of a boom box couldn't get Lila to do. "Or you could let me wear your embroidered jeans tomorrow," she quickly added.

"I guess," Lila said, sounding irritated. "But then I get to listen to what I want first."

Ellen suddenly sat up. "Does that boom box come with earphones, Jessica?" she asked.

"Yeah," she said. "They're packed in a little compartment in the back of it."

Ellen gave Lila a challenging glance. "Tell

you what, Jessica: I'll do your kitchen duty tomorrow if you let me listen to it first—with headphones."

"What?" Lila said, a look of disbelief on her face. "Then nobody else can listen to it."

"Hey, that's not fair," Caroline protested.

"Why not?" Ellen said. "If I'm willing to do the work, why shouldn't I get to listen to it however I want?"

Ellen, Lila, and Caroline started squabbling over who should get to do what. Jessica laughed to herself. *Bringing the boom box was a stroke of genius,* she mused.

But then Jessica looked toward Elizabeth's empty cot and began to have second thoughts. She didn't think Elizabeth would approve of her using the box to bribe her friends to do her chores.

Her thoughts were interrupted by Brooke Dennis coming over to her. "Jessica, it's so boring sitting around here with no lights and nothing to do. If you'll let me listen to your boom box for an hour tonight, I'll weed the strawberry patch for you tomorrow afternoon," she offered.

Jessica had been dreading bending over in

the hot sun to pluck weeds out of the dirt—not to mention dealing with the earthworms and other crawly things she would probably run across. Her conscience reminded her of Elizabeth, but it was no contest.

"OK," Jessica agreed happily. Soon she had a crowd of eager friends around her. Jessica had never felt so popular as she traded away the rest of the weekend's chores.

It was a beautiful, warm evening, but Elizabeth barely noticed it as she walked around the peach orchard, wondering what to do about Jessica. Her twin was famous for not thinking through the consequences of her actions. Jessica's impulses had gotten Elizabeth into more scrapes than she wanted to remember.

A noise from one of the peach trees caught Elizabeth's attention. She squinted in the darkness and saw a pair of khaki-clad legs standing on a ladder braced against the tree trunk. Rustling noises came from the leaves that hid the top half of the person.

"Mrs. Arnette?" Elizabeth said tentatively.

There was some more rustling from above, and then Mrs. Arnette descended the ladder.

"Oh—hello, Elizabeth," she said. "I didn't expect to see any students out here at this hour."

"I just felt like taking a walk," Elizabeth explained. "Um . . . do you need some help?"

Mrs. Arnette blushed. "No, Elizabeth, thank you. I couldn't—uh, that is, something came up earlier today, and I was, uh, prevented from finishing all the tasks I should have gotten to. There are peaches on the menu for breakfast tomorrow, and I didn't want you children to be disappointed, so . . ."

"Picking peaches can be hard work," Elizabeth added gravely, trying very hard not to smile. "Are you sure you wouldn't like some help?"

"It's very kind of you to offer, Elizabeth, but no thank you," Mrs. Arnette said.

"OK. Good night," Elizabeth said as she walked away. She smiled to herself. It was nice to know that teachers could have just as much trouble finishing assignments as students have.

As Elizabeth headed back to the bunkhouse, she passed the hand pump, and to her surprise she saw Lila struggling with it.

"Stupid pump!" Lila cried in frustration,

slamming down a water glass and examining one of her nails.

Elizabeth stifled a giggle and made her way to the bunkhouse door.

As she entered the bunkhouse she saw a bunch of girls clustered around Jessica's cot. But before she could go over to her twin and find out what was going on, Amy and Julie came over to her and motioned her outside.

"Elizabeth! I'm glad you're back. We want to go over to the boys' bunkhouse and spy on them," Amy said. "If we can catch them eating potato chips or playing Nintendo, we'll instantly win the bet."

"But we've already lost the bet," Elizabeth said sadly. "Jessica brought the boom box."

Julie said, "Yes, but she hasn't used it yet. I don't think that really breaks the rules of the bet."

Just then Lila edged past them, carrying a glass of water. Elizabeth watched in amazement as Lila went over to Jessica's cot and handed her the water.

"Here you go," Lila muttered. "Just what you asked for."

"Thank you, Lila," Jessica said.

Elizabeth could not believe what she was seeing. *Lila* was serving Jessica water?

"I can't believe my eyes. What in the world is going on?" Elizabeth asked.

Amy grinned. "Your sister has decided to let everyone have a turn listening to the boom box—with the earphones—in exchange for doing some of her chores."

"I couldn't believe it, either," Julie added.

"Sometimes I absolutely cannot believe Jessica is my twin," Elizabeth said angrily. "She's gone too far this time."

"Maybe you should tell Ms. Shepard about the boom box," Julie suggested. "That would teach Jessica a lesson."

"No," Elizabeth said. "I couldn't do that. But maybe I can convince her to—"

At that moment a hoarse scream came from the direction of the peach orchard.

All the girls in the bunkhouse leaped up.

"Who was that?" Brooke asked.

"It sounded like Mrs. Arnette!" Elizabeth shouted as the girls ran outside.

Lumbering toward them as fast as she

could was Mrs. Arnette. Her normally neat bun was disheveled, and she was jumping and brushing at herself as she ran.

Ms. Shepard had come out of the main house when she heard the scream. "What's wrong?" Ms. Shepard asked. "Calm down. Tell me what happened."

"Wasps!" Mrs. Arnette said frantically. "I was up in a peach tree trying to pick some peaches. I reached up and all of a sudden—" Mrs. Arnette shuddered and compulsively brushed off her arms. "All of a sudden, I felt these insects—dozens of them—swarming around me."

"Did you get stung?" Ms. Shepard asked.

"No," Mrs. Arnette said, sinking down onto a bench outside the farmhouse. "Thank heavens."

"It's OK," Ms. Shepard told Ms. Emburg, who walked over from the farmhouse with a first-aid kit. "She stirred up a wasps' nest, but she didn't get stung."

"Poor thing," Ms. Emburg said, sitting down next to Mrs. Arnette and putting an arm around her. "That can be frightening."

"Oh, it was," Mrs. Arnette said, heaving a huge sigh. "There were so many horrible insects! Hundreds, even thousands!"

Just then Coach Cassels came running up. "Is everything all right?" he asked.

"I bumped into a wasps' nest in the peach orchard," Mrs. Arnette told him. "All of a sudden there were millions of insects flying around me. Billions! All buzzing away!"

Elizabeth couldn't resist a smile as she heard the story get more and more dramatic with each telling.

"You should lie down," Ms. Shepard said. "Why don't I make you some chamomile tea?"

"What I'd really like is some freshly brewed coffee and a good hot bath," Mrs. Arnette said wistfully. "Darn this place," Elizabeth heard her mutter as she walked away.

As soon as she had gone the girls began laughing uncontrollably.

"Something makes me think Mrs. Arnette isn't having the exciting educational experience she told us to expect," Maria joked.

* * *

"Are you sure this is a good idea?" Elizabeth whispered to Amy later that night. "What if the boys catch us?"

"They won't," Amy assured her. "We'll be really quiet."

"I can't wait to catch them breaking the rules," Julie said.

"I bet we catch Charlie with a Snickers bar," Maria added. "Have you ever seen him go a whole day without eating at least two?"

"OK," Elizabeth said, stifling a laugh. "Let's go!"

The four girls crept across the yard, then inched along the back wall of the boys' bunkhouse. When they turned the corner they could see a yellow glow coming from one of the windows.

"Look! They have light!" Elizabeth whispered excitedly. "That means a flashlight!"

"I told you spying on them was a good idea," Amy hissed. She rushed forward and stopped under the screened window. Ever so slowly she raised her head until her eyes were just above the sill. She looked for a moment, then silently motioned the others over. "It's not a flashlight. They're using a lantern," she whispered.

Elizabeth peeked over the sill.

"No, Magic Johnson's the best basketball player ever," Todd was arguing inside the bunkhouse.

"I still vote for Larry Bird," Ken said.

There was a creak from one of the cots as someone turned over. "I don't know about you guys, but I hate living like a pioneer," Winston Egbert said.

"No joke," Aaron remarked. "Life without cable TV stinks."

"When I get home I'm going to fall on the ground and worship the dishwasher," Randy Mason grumbled. "I hated washing all those dishes tonight."

"My back hurts," Todd complained.

The girls had heard enough. All four of them quietly crept away from the boys' bunkhouse. The moon was shining brightly as they crossed the courtyard, and they made it back to the door of their own bunkhouse in no time at all.

"The boys are just about ready to crack," Maria said with a grin. "This is great!"

"Wait till we tell the others," Elizabeth said. "Maybe this will convince them to stick to the rules and leave the boom box alone."

But when Elizabeth swung open the bunkhouse door, she saw that it was already too late. By the light of a candle at Jessica's bedside, Elizabeth could see her twin listening to the boom box through the earphones.

The girls had lost the bet.

Nine

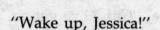

"Wake up, Jessica!"

Jessica grumbled and rolled over, pulling the blanket over her head. She had slept badly on the lumpy, sagging cot, and she wanted nothing more than a few more hours of peaceful sleep.

"Jessica!"

"What *what* WHAT?" Jessica growled, sitting up and throwing off the blanket.

Lila was sitting on the edge of her bed, grinning. "It's raining!"

"Huh?" Jessica could hear the raindrops pattering on the wooden roof of the bunkhouse, but she couldn't figure out why Lila would wake her up to tell her this.

"Didn't you hear what I said, Jessica? It's raining! That means we can't go outside today and do more horrible farm chores! Isn't it great?"

Just then the door to the bunkhouse opened, and Mrs. Arnette and Ms. Shepard came in.

"Good morning, girls!" Ms. Shepard called cheerfully. "It's six-thirty. Rise and shine!"

The girls stirred sleepily in their cots. Mrs. Arnette waited until most of them had opened their eyes before she spoke. "Girls, I've got an announcement to make."

Lila and Jessica shared a knowing glance.

"It's raining outside, as you can probably hear. But don't worry. I can assure you that none of your farm fun will be canceled."

"All the animals still need to be fed, the horses' stalls have to be cleaned out, and the goats and cows need to be milked," Ms. Shepard added. "Plus the food has to be prepared and the dishes washed. So everything will go on as usual. Almost everything, that is—those of you who were scheduled to weed the vegetable and strawberry patch will spend some time indoors learning how to weave and knit."

"The boys, too?" Julie questioned from her bed.

"Boys, too," Ms. Shepard confirmed. "It's true that back in the pioneer days men tended to do certain kinds of work and women usually did other kinds, but we want each of you to be familiar with all of the chores that had to be done on a pioneer farm."

"This is awful!" Lila cried as soon as the teachers left the room. "We actually have to go out in that disgusting weather? My new suede boots are going to be ruined."

Suddenly Jessica remembered the deals she had made the night before. "Lila, I feel *so* sorry for you," she said, trying not to smile.

"What do you mean, for me?" Lila asked suspiciously.

"You may have to go outside and be a farm slave, but I don't," Jessica said with a smirk. "Brooke and Caroline are doing most of my morning chores, and Ellen and Belinda are doing *all* of my afternoon chores." She stretched lazily and fluffed up her pillow before she lay down again. "So I can relax in the bunkhouse most of the day—after all, Mrs. Arnette did say that when our work was done, we could do whatever we wanted."

Lila glared at Jessica, but said nothing.

This is great, Jessica thought. *Maybe I can get Elizabeth and Steven to do all my chores at home, too!*

"How are those biscuits?" Ms. Shepard asked at breakfast, standing up and surveying the hungry sixth-graders.

Elizabeth was spreading homemade blackberry preserves on her second biscuit. "Fantastic," she answered.

"Mmph! Good!" Charlie seconded from across the dining room, his mouth full.

"Remember, tomorrow morning everyone will be expected to help put together a great Sunday breakfast, and then afterward we'll have a hayride," Ms. Shepard reminded them.

"That sounds fun," Julie commented to Elizabeth.

Caroline Pearce came over with a dish of peaches and sat down at Elizabeth and Julie's table. "Have you taken a good look at Mrs. Arnette this morning?" she asked.

Elizabeth glanced at the teacher, who was sitting nearby. "She looks a little tired," Elizabeth said.

Caroline nodded. "And have you ever seen her hair so messy? It looks like a little kid did her bun this morning."

"Look at the way she's rubbing her eyes," Julie noted. "She keeps talking about coffee."

"Coach Cassels isn't doing so hot either," Caroline confided. "Look at the way he's getting up from his chair. I heard he threw his back out, chopping wood yesterday."

Elizabeth laughed. "How do you hear these things, Caroline?"

Caroline shrugged. "I have my sources," she said.

"Maybe you should have made a bet with the teachers instead of with the boys, Elizabeth," Julie said with a smile. "It's the teachers who seem to be falling apart!"

"Teachers just don't have the stuff pioneers are made of," Caroline declared.

Elizabeth laughed and stood up. "Ready to hit the barn?" she asked Amy.

"Let's go," Amy said, standing up.

"But don't you want to hear about—" Caroline began, a hint of a whine in her voice.

"Sorry, we've got a lot of work to do," Elizabeth said.

As they went through the doorway Elizabeth turned around, and she had to smile. Caroline had found a place where her gossip skills would be appreciated—at the Unicorn's table.

"Look at the way they eat," Lila said, wrinkling her nose. "Now I know why they're called pigs."

Jessica poured another bucket of slop into the pigs' trough. This was the one chore she hadn't been able to convince any of her friends to do for her. She also figured that Mrs. Arnette might get suspicious if she stayed in the bunkhouse the whole day.

"Feeding the pigs isn't as bad as I thought it would be," Jessica admitted. "The big ones are ugly and noisy, but the babies are adorable."

Mandy Miller bent down and scooped up a chubby pink piglet. "He's so cute. I'd love to take him home to show my family."

"Don't forget what happened to Lila when she tried to take an egg from its mother," Jessica warned, laughing.

"Shut up," Lila muttered through clenched teeth. "And don't get any of that disgusting stuff on my jeans."

Jessica chuckled. She was enjoying wearing Lila's new, expensive jeans with the elaborate embroidery down the side of each leg. "Well, I'll try, Lila, but I can't help it if the pigs bump into me, can I?"

Mandy was stroking the wriggling piglet. "Look at his little corkscrew tail," she cooed.

"Can I hold him?" Jessica asked.

Mandy nodded and carefully gave the animal to Jessica.

Jessica cuddled the piglet, who had stopped wriggling. "Look! I think he likes me!"

"Yeah, he likes you all right, Jessica," Charlie called out as he and Winston pushed a wheelbarrow past the pigpen.

"Jessica's got a new boyfriend," Winston called out loudly.

"And he's a real pig," Charlie added with a laugh.

Jessica glared at the boys. "Get lost," she snapped.

But Charlie stepped over the thigh-high fence surrounding the pigpen and grabbed the piglet out of Jessica's arms.

"Give him back to me!" Jessica insisted, lunging in Charlie's direction.

But Charlie backed away, out of Jessica's reach. He held the piglet up in the air. "Hey, look at him, Winston!"

Winston hopped over the fence, too, and took the piglet, who had begun to struggle again. "He's an active little guy, isn't he? I can barely keep a grip on him—"

The piglet squealed shrilly and then squirmed out of Winston's grasp, landing safely on the ground and running back to its mother. But Winston lost his balance and fell backward, landing in the pigs' trough. Pigs squealed and scattered in all directions.

Jessica, Lila, and Mandy all cracked up. "And they say *pigs* are disgusting animals!" Jessica shouted triumphantly.

*   *   *

Across the barnyard, Elizabeth and Amy had nearly finished mucking out Slug's stall.

"You're a good horse, yes you are," Elizabeth said, reaching up to scratch behind the horse's ears. "It's stopped raining, so maybe I can ride you this morning after I finish the other stalls."

"I can see you're in love," Amy teased. She was sweeping the stall floor with a handmade straw broom.

Elizabeth reddened. "He's irresistible, isn't he?" she said.

Just then Maria poked her head into the barn. "Hi, guys. Ms. Shepard wants everyone to come over to the main house."

"Bye, Slug," Elizabeth whispered, and then closed his stall and headed over to the big old farmhouse.

"Everyone," Ms. Shepard said when the class had gathered, "I want to commend you all for working so hard in such muddy conditions. That shows you've all got real pioneer spirit. As a special treat, we've got some freshly made oatmeal cookies!"

Some of the kids let out rowdy whoops and stamped their feet on the wide floor-planks.

"I have one other announcement before you start to eat," Ms. Shepard continued over the noise. "The cows need to be rounded up, and I want to know if there's anyone here who can ride a horse."

Elizabeth, Ellen, Lila, Maria, and Ginny Lu all raised their hands.

"I'll only need two helpers. How about Elizabeth and Maria? Want to help me?" Ms. Shepard asked.

"I'd love to!" Elizabeth said, excited.

"Me, too!" Maria agreed.

As the three of them headed for the barn, the sun peeked out for the first time that day. Elizabeth chose to ride Slug. Maria picked a bay mare named Sally.

"We'll start out in the north pasture," Ms. Shepard said, saddling a spotted Appaloosa. "We're dealing with a small herd of cows, so it shouldn't take long." She explained to them how they should circle around behind the herd and get them to move in the direction of the corral.

"Ready?" Elizabeth asked Maria excitedly when they were mounted. Maria nodded. "OK, then. Let's go!" Elizabeth tapped Slug's sides gently with her heels, and off they went. With Ms. Shepard in the lead, they cantered toward the pasture.

Although Elizabeth had never herded cattle before, Slug seemed to be an expert. With just a slight nudge from Elizabeth, the horse cut off a cow from one side and then sidestepped around to the cow's other side. Several of the cattle started heading in the right direction.

"You and Maria make great cowgirls! We're almost finished," Ms. Shepard said a short while later. "And it's a good thing, too," she said, looking up at the sky, which had again turned an ominous charcoal gray. "I think we're in for some more rain."

"There's just one straggler over there," Elizabeth told Ms. Shepard. She pointed to a small brown cow grazing near an oak tree about three hundred feet away. "I'll get that one." Propelling Slug into a gallop, Elizabeth hurried after the animal.

Suddenly Elizabeth saw an enormous bolt of lightning strike the oak tree, splitting a thick branch off the main trunk. A tremendous crack of thunder shook the air and the ground. Slug, terrified, reared up with a frantic whinny and leaped to his left. The frightened cow ran toward the rest of the herd.

Elizabeth was very scared, but she managed to stay on Slug's back. Holding the reins firmly, she tried to calm the horse. Large raindrops began to splatter her face. "Easy, boy!" she called, her voice trembling.

Suddenly another bolt of lightning flashed nearby and thunder roared once more. Slug reared up again, and then took off in a wild charge—away from Maria, Ms. Shepard, and the farm, and straight toward a dense clump of trees at the edge of the pasture!

Elizabeth cried out and clung desperately to Slug's neck. She had never been so frightened in her entire life!

"Where are they?" Mrs. Arnette asked, pacing back and forth and biting her nails. "Oh, I hope they're safe."

Jessica worriedly peered out the bunkhouse window. She knew Elizabeth was a good rider, but the storm was getting worse.

"No one should be outside in this storm," Brooke commented, shivering as she looked at the treetops bending under the strong wind.

"Maybe they found a building to take shelter in," Amy said as she joined Brooke and Jessica at the window.

Jessica stared out the window for another few minutes. The rain was pelting down heavily, and the thunder was getting louder. "Shouldn't we go out and look for them?" she asked Mrs. Arnette.

Mrs. Arnette shook her head. "It would be too dangerous. We'll simply have to wait."

Suddenly Amy shouted, "Someone's coming!"

The bunkhouse door opened and in walked Maria. She was dripping wet and obviously frightened.

"Where's my sister?" Jessica demanded, hurrying over to her.

Maria started to cry. Mrs. Arnette put an arm around Maria's shoulders. "Elizabeth's horse got scared and bolted toward the woods," Maria explained between sobs. "And Ms. Shepard went after her!"

Jessica felt dizzy all of a sudden. She sank

down onto a cot. She felt terrible for having been so awful to Elizabeth lately.

Oh, please let her be all right, Jessica repeated to herself over and over again. *I'll never fight with her again! Please let her walk through that door right now!* But the door stayed shut.

And outside, the storm raged on.

Ten

◇

"Slug, stop!" Elizabeth shouted as she struggled to stay on the racing horse. "Whoa! *Stop!*"

The horse had been running at full speed for at least ten minutes, and Elizabeth no longer knew where she was.

"*Please*, Slug," she pleaded, the tears on her face mixing with the rain.

After another few minutes, the worst of the storm was over. As the sound of the thunder receded, the horse slowed his pace and eventually came to a stop.

"Good boy," Elizabeth murmured, her face still pressed against the horse's neck. She sat up and tried to get a better grip on the reins, but her hands were shaking.

Elizabeth took a deep breath. "Everything's going to be all right," she said, as much to herself as to the horse.

She decided to turn around and try to go back the way she had come, hoping that she would recognize some of the clumps of trees she had passed on the wild ride. But Slug wouldn't turn around, no matter how much she tugged on the reins.

Finally she let Slug walk in the direction he wanted to go. *Animals have a good sense of direction*, Elizabeth told herself. *Maybe he knows how to get home.*

Five minutes later they crossed a small stream, and Elizabeth saw a white farmhouse in front of her. She sighed with relief; a farmhouse meant shelter and people. She was safe!

The horse trotted up to the old barn that stood alongside the farmhouse and stopped in front of the closed door. Elizabeth, puzzled at Slug's strange behavior, dismounted and tied the horse's reins to a nearby fence post. Then she made her way to the door of the farmhouse and knocked.

A tall, thin, bearded man answered the door.

"Um, hi," Elizabeth began tentatively. "I'm Elizabeth Wakefield, and I'm a little lost."

The man surveyed her, and Elizabeth realized how bedraggled she must look. "Were you out walking in this storm?" the man asked, opening the screen door.

"No," she said. "I was riding a horse—that horse over there," she said, pointing to Slug, "over on the Sweet Valley College pioneer farm. When the storm started, the horse got scared by the thunder and he bolted."

To Elizabeth's surprise, the man came outside and peered at the horse more closely. "Slug?" he said. From over by the barn, Slug looked up and whinnied.

"You know him?" Elizabeth asked.

The man chuckled. "Sure do. He was foaled here on my farm. He's a good horse, but he's always been scared of thunder, just like his mama. I'm sorry you got such a nasty surprise."

"I'm OK," Elizabeth reassured him.

"Tell you what—I'll take you inside and hand you over to my wife, and then I'll put Slug here in the barn to warm up."

"Thanks, Mr., uh . . ."

"Lowes, Ed Lowes."

"Mrs. Arnette should have let me go after Elizabeth," Jessica said bitterly, pounding her pillow.

"Try not to worry, Jessica," Amy said comfortingly. "The rain looks like it's letting up. I'm sure Ms. Shepard will find her."

"You know, Jessica, I bet Elizabeth is doing this on purpose to make you worry about her," Ellen said. She was stretched out on her bed, her eyes closed. "She was really mad at you before. She's probably just trying to get back at you."

Jessica jumped up, furious. "How dare you say that about my sister? Elizabeth would *never* do anything like that!"

Ellen opened her eyes and looked at Jessica. "Take it easy, Jess. I'm sorry. I just meant that I'm sure Elizabeth's going to be all right."

Jessica resumed pacing around the bunkhouse, passing by the window every few seconds. She kept remembering how she had ruined Elizabeth's bet. More than anything, she wanted the chance to tell Elizabeth how sorry she was. A tear rolled down her cheek.

Lila came over to her. "Hey, Jessica, want to listen to the radio? The deejay is interviewing one of the bands that's going to play at Aid the People later today, and—" She caught sight of Jessica's tears. "Don't cry, Jess," Lila said awkwardly. "Ellen's right. Elizabeth is going to be fine. You'll see."

Jessica gazed out the window. To her dismay, the rain had picked up again and was falling heavily. *If only it would stop raining!* she thought miserably.

"Sit right here, dear," Mrs. Lowes said, pulling out a chair at the kitchen table. The room was warm and the smell of something delicious came from the oven.

"Thank you," Elizabeth replied, and sank down gratefully. "I'm sorry I'm dripping water on your floor."

"Oh, don't worry about that," Mrs. Lowes said with a smile. "We've had pigs, chickens, and geese through here, so you can be sure the floor's seen a lot worse! Here, let me get you a cup of tea while I see about getting you some dry clothes. You're a bit taller than my daughter, Melinda. Still, I think I can find something for you to wear."

"I really appreciate your help," Elizabeth said.

"Ed said you're staying at the pioneer farm," Mrs. Lowes said as she poured hot water into a mug and added a tea bag.

"That's right. But only for the weekend," Elizabeth said. "I'm from Sweet Valley Middle School. We're on a field trip."

"I thought you looked a little young to be a college student," Mrs. Lowes teased, setting the mug down in front of Elizabeth. "I'll be right back," she added, then went upstairs.

Elizabeth sipped the warm tea and began to relax a little. It felt good to be safe and out of the rain. She only hoped that Jessica and the others back at the farm weren't too worried about her.

The back door opened, and Mr. Lowes came in. He slipped off his muddy boots and left them by the door. "Slug's all taken care of. The storm's picking up again, though, and the winds are pretty strong. As soon as it eases up a bit I'll take you over in the truck, and I'll bring Slug over in the horse trailer tomorrow."

"Thank you," Elizabeth said. "Do you think we'll be able to go back soon? Everyone must be wondering what happened to me."

Mr. Lowes went over to the stove and started to fix himself a cup of coffee. "I think we'd better stay here for an hour or two," he said. "The road between here and the pioneer farm is dirt, and so it'll be all mud by now. With the high winds on top of that, I'd rather wait until I'm sure it's safe." He looked over at Elizabeth, concern on his face. "I do wish we could call them and tell them you're safe. But as you probably know, they don't have a phone."

Just then Mrs. Lowes came back in the room. She handed Elizabeth a denim skirt and a pink polo shirt. "Try these on, dear. The bathroom's up at the top of the stairs. If they fit, you can just leave your wet clothes in the tub."

Elizabeth went upstairs and shed her wet things. Luckily, the clothes fit her perfectly. She glanced into the mirror. Her hair was still damp and she was a little pale, but she felt more like her usual self.

"Those fit well," Mrs. Lowes said when Elizabeth came downstairs again.

"Will your daughter mind me wearing her clothes?" Elizabeth asked.

"Oh, not at all," Mrs. Lowes replied. "Melinda has closets full of clothes. Her favorite hobby is shopping."

"My sister is like that, too," Elizabeth said with a smile.

"Want to go downstairs and join the party now?" Mrs. Lowes asked.

"Party?" Elizabeth asked.

Mrs. Lowes laughed. "I'm sorry, I guess with all the excitement we forgot to tell you! Today is Melinda's birthday. She and her friends are downstairs having a birthday party."

"How old is she?" Elizabeth asked.

"Twelve."

"Twelve! That's the same age I am!"

Mrs. Lowes grinned. "Then you two should have a lot in common. Just follow me." She led the way to a room filled with music, balloons, and lots of kids her age.

"Melinda," Mrs. Lowes called, "I brought you another guest."

"Hi," Melinda said, looking at Elizabeth curiously.

"I'm Elizabeth Wakefield. I'm visiting the pioneer farm with my class, and I got lost in the storm."

"I'm Melinda," she said with a big smile. "Well, I'm glad you're here. Come on over and have some cake." As the two girls made their way to a table at the other side of the rec room, Melinda started to introduce Elizabeth around. "Elizabeth, this is Jenny, Pam, and Rick. Guys, this is Elizabeth Wakefield. The storm blew her over here from the pioneer farm."

"Are all these kids from your class?" Elizabeth asked as she munched on some chips.

Melinda nodded. "Yes. We're all in sixth grade at Corona Valley Middle School."

Just then Mrs. Lowes came down the stairs with a batch of warm, delicious-smelling chocolate chip cookies, and Elizabeth recognized the smell from earlier in the kitchen. She was happy to accept a tall glass of milk and some cookies, which Melinda vowed were "the best in the county."

Elizabeth had to agree. And as she ate and listened to a Coco song, she realized how glad she was to be in a safe, warm, *modern* home.

Eleven

◆

"Come on, Jessica, you have to eat something," Lila urged, holding out a slice of bread covered with peanut butter. "You didn't touch your lunch."

Most of the sixth-graders were out doing their afternoon chores, but Jessica, Amy, Lila, Ellen, Maria, and Julie were sitting in the dining room, waiting for news about Elizabeth.

Jessica shook her head. "I'm not hungry. What time is it?"

Maria looked at the old-fashioned key-wound clock in the corner. "Almost two o'clock."

"Elizabeth's been missing for over three hours!" Jessica wailed. "Oh, I just know something terrible's happened to her."

"I'm sure she's OK," Maria said, though she didn't look like she was one hundred percent sure.

"Come on, Jessica. Have some peanut butter," Lila urged. "It'll cheer you up."

Jessica said nothing. She felt numb all over. *I wish I'd never fought with her*, she kept thinking. *Oh, Lizzie, please be all right.*

The door opened and Jessica looked up. A dripping wet Ms. Shepard was at the door. She was back! A mixture of hope and fear raced through Jessica.

"I found her!" Ms. Shepard exclaimed.

"*Lizzie!*" Jessica shrieked, springing up from her chair and racing over to the door, just as Elizabeth stepped into the room. Jessica threw her arms around her sister. "Oh, Lizzie, I'm so glad you're back!"

"Me, too," Elizabeth said, returning Jessica's hug.

"I was so worried!" Jessica told her.

"I was, too," Elizabeth said. "Slug got scared by the thunder and took off. I was terrified I was going to fall off or be struck by lightning."

"You're not hurt, are you?" Jessica asked.

"No," Elizabeth replied. "I was lucky."

Jessica stepped back and surveyed her sister. *Hmm, no scratches or bruises*, she said to herself.

"Lizzie," Jessica began, "where did you get those clothes?"

"Tell us everything that happened," Amy interrupted.

"Hang on," Elizabeth said. "Let me sit down. I'm pretty tired."

"No wonder you're tired," Maria said sympathetically. "Getting dragged all over in a rainstorm by a terrified horse . . ."

Elizabeth grinned. "That's not really why I'm so tired. My problem is that I danced too much."

"Danced?" Maria said.

Jessica gave her twin a worried look. Maybe Elizabeth was so scared she had cracked.

"It's a long story," Elizabeth answered with a smile.

Jessica put her arm around her twin's shoulders. "I think you should go back to the bunkhouse and lie down for a while, Lizzie. But before you go . . ." Jessica took a deep breath and looked Elizabeth straight in the eye. "I just wanted to tell you one thing. I'm sorry for all those horrible things I said to you. I know the whole fight was my fault. I should never have been so selfish about the computer and everything."

"Oh, Jess, I could never stay mad at you anyway," Elizabeth said, her eyes bright. "It wasn't all your fault, you know. I could have been more understanding."

"I promise I'll be the best sister in the world from now on," Jessica said earnestly.

"I don't want the world's best sister," Elizabeth replied, hugging Jessica again. "I just want you."

"So tell us everything," Amy said when they were all settled with mugs of tea in the big kitchen.

"Yeah," Jessica said. "Was it awful? Did you see any wild animals? Was your life in danger?"

Elizabeth smiled. "Not really, no, and no," she answered. "Except for the part when Slug was running full-speed into the woods. That was pretty scary."

"Did you get lost?" Amy asked.

"I did, but luckily Slug knew where he was. He took me to his home."

Amy looked puzzled.

"This isn't Slug's first home," Elizabeth explained. "He was born on a farm a few miles away. Anyway, that's where he took me. A family named Lowes lives there."

"What happened when you got there?" Jessica asked.

Elizabeth grinned. "I was invited to a birthday party."

"What?" several girls asked at once.

"The Loweses' daughter, Melinda, was having her twelfth-birthday party," Elizabeth explained. "While we waited for the storm to die down, I went downstairs and joined the party."

"So that's where you were dancing," Maria said.

"I'm glad to know it really happened, Lizzie," Jessica said seriously. "I thought you had gone crazy."

Elizabeth smiled. "The party was a lot of fun. There was lots of great food and a few really cute boys. And the music was great."

Jessica shook her head. "All that time I was

worried sick about you, and where were you? Off having fun at a party!"

"Wait a minute," Amy said. "Did you say there was music there?"

Elizabeth nodded. "Melinda is a big Melody Powers fan. She must have every CD Melody Powers ever made."

"So you used electricity," Amy said. "What about the bet with the boys?"

"But she wasn't here at the farm," Maria argued. "I don't think it should count."

"No, I think Amy's right," Elizabeth said. "Pioneers didn't listen to CDs. I could try to keep it a secret, but since it *is* my bet, I might as well be honest. I guess I'll have to make that speech after all."

"I'll help you write it, Lizzie," Jessica said.

Elizabeth groaned. "This is going to be so humiliating. But a bet's a bet. Well, I guess there's only one thing left to do."

"What?" Jessica asked.

"Go to the boys' bunkhouse and admit defeat," Elizabeth said.

Elizabeth could hear loud voices and laughter coming from the boys' bunkhouse. "It was great of you guys to come with me," she told Amy, Julie, and Jessica, "but you don't have to come inside if you don't want."

"You can't get rid of us so easily," Jessica said with a smile.

"I wonder what's going on in there," Julie said, her brow furrowed. "They're awfully noisy."

"It sounds like they're having a party," Jessica said.

"My life is one party after another," Elizabeth joked.

Jessica held up her hand. "Wait a sec. I hear music!"

Elizabeth pricked up her ears. She heard music, too!

"Let's check it out," Amy suggested, going over to the window the girls had peered in the night before.

"Hey, look!" Julie said. "They *do* have music. And that isn't all!"

Inside, a dozen boys were gathered around a portable TV. And everyone was drinking soda and snacking on pretzels and potato chips— even Coach Cassels!

"To think that I was going to go in there and admit defeat!" Elizabeth said with a laugh.

"I can't believe this!" Jessica said. "Do you realize what they're watching? It's the Aid the People concert!"

"I vote we go in and catch them in the act," Amy said.

"Yeah!" Jessica said.

Elizabeth strode to the bunkhouse door and flung it open. Suddenly the only noise was a blaring commercial.

"What are you doing?" she demanded fiercely, trying not to smile.

Coach Cassels attempted to hide a handful of pretzels behind his back. None of the boys said anything.

"I can't believe you guys!" Julie said.

"This is a really dinky TV. The sound's awful," Ken meekly pointed out.

"Well, since you guys blew the bet and all," Jessica said, cheerfully settling herself in front of the TV, "do you mind if I watch this? The sound is pretty awful, though. You know what? We should bring over my boom box—"

Elizabeth, Amy, and Julie turned and glared at Jessica.

"You brought a boom box?" Todd asked.

"So *you* lost the bet!" Aaron shouted. He

flung his arms in the air and began to do a victory dance.

"Wait a minute!" Jessica shouted. She marched over to Aaron and grabbed his arm. "What's this?"

"A watch," Aaron said. "Didn't pioneers have watches?"

"Maybe they did, but not *digital* ones!" Jessica pointed out triumphantly.

Todd looked at Elizabeth and grinned. "It looks like we both lost," he said. "I guess it's a draw."

Jessica nudged Elizabeth. "Hey, Lizzie, since nobody is going to have to make a speech on Monday, how about watching a little TV?"

"The Aid the People concert?" Elizabeth asked.

Jessica nodded.

Elizabeth smiled. "All right, all right. Go get the boom box and everyone from our bunkhouse!"

Twelve

◇

"Hey, Elizabeth!" Maria called as she burst into the bunkhouse Sunday morning. "The hay wagon's outside. And guess who's helping pull it!"

"Slug?" Elizabeth said.

"Right!"

"I'll be out in just a second," Elizabeth said, smiling. She rummaged around in her bag for the lump of sugar she had saved from breakfast so that she could give Slug a treat. Sticking it in the pocket of her denim jacket, she ran outside.

"Hey, Slug, I'm glad Mr. Lowes brought you back," she said, feeding the big horse the sugar. His soft lips nuzzled her palm as he ate it. Elizabeth reached up and patted his nose, and Slug neighed.

"All aboard!" Ms. Shepard called, and Elizabeth scrambled up onto a pile of itchy hay. She settled down next to Todd, who had pieces of hay in his hair.

"Having fun?" he asked as the wagon lurched forward.

"Maria's elbow is in my ribs, Jessica keeps sitting on my foot, and all this hay is making me sneeze," Elizabeth said happily. "I love it!" As she spoke she glanced over at Jessica, who was sitting close to Aaron. *I have a feeling Jessica likes hayrides, too,* she thought with a smile.

"I'm glad we called off that dumb bet," Todd said. "I kind of feel like I said things I didn't really mean."

"Me, too," Elizabeth said. "After all, boys are *almost* as good as girls."

"What?" Todd said.

Elizabeth laughed, and Todd tossed a handful of hay at her. She grinned and threw a handful right back at him.

"Hay fight! Hay fight!" someone said. Soon the air was full of flying hay and laughter.

*   *   *

"Oof!" Elizabeth said as she lifted her suitcase off her bunk. "Why are suitcases always heavier at the end of a trip?"

"Are you sure you're not trying to smuggle Slug out?" Amy asked teasingly as she zipped her own suitcase shut.

"I did try," Elizabeth said with a laugh. "But his tail stuck out!" Lugging her bag over to the door, Elizabeth saw that Jessica was lying on her bunk and talking with Lila. "Are you packed, Jess?"

Jessica nodded. "I packed last night. Boy, am I going to be glad to get home to electric lights and running water."

"I hope I never see another outhouse in my life," Lila said dramatically.

"Didn't you enjoy pioneer life at least a little?" Elizabeth asked her twin.

Jessica shrugged. "It was sort of fun, but the pioneers worked too hard."

Amy scoffed. "*You* hardly worked at all. Unless lounging around on a cot is considered a chore."

Elizabeth sighed. "I have to say, it's a lot easier to get milk and eggs out of the refrigerator than directly from the animal!"

"I guess this weekend made us all realize how easy we have it," Amy said.

Jessica laughed. "Yeah—this was a lot tougher than Mrs. Arnette's usual assignments!"

"We're back!" Jessica exclaimed, rushing into the Wakefields' kitchen.

Mr. Wakefield put down the Sunday comics and smiled at his daughter. "So, how was pioneer life?"

Jessica gave him a kiss on the cheek. "Great . . . but not as great as being home!"

Elizabeth entered the kitchen, dropped her suitcase, and hugged her father. Mrs. Wakefield followed behind her, carrying Jessica's suitcase. "Jessica, what in the world do you have in here?" she asked. "Rocks?"

Jessica had forgotten about the boom box, which she had wrapped in her bathrobe for the trip home. Rushing over to her mother, she took the suitcase. "Oh, sorry, Mom. I'll take this upstairs."

"Not so fast, Jessica."

Halfway to the stairs, Jessica stopped and turned around guiltily.

Mrs. Wakefield crossed her arms and

looked at her daughter. "Jessica, do you have what I think you have in there?"

"Well, I, uh, sort of forgot I wasn't allowed to bring this," Jessica said, setting the boom box on the kitchen table. "How did you know?"

Mrs. Wakefield smiled in spite of herself. "Steven wanted to use it, and when I couldn't find it anywhere I figured out what must have happened," she said.

"I'm sorry," Jessica said sincerely. "And I'll never do it again."

"I hope not," Mrs. Wakefield said.

"She won't have the chance to—at least not for a few weeks," Mr. Wakefield said. "I'm going to take it to the office for a while."

Jessica stared at her father. "*You* want to listen to a boom box?"

Mr. Wakefield grinned. "I do listen to music once in a while," he said. "They did have rock and roll when I was growing up, you know."

"But I wanted to—" Jessica began.

"It won't be so bad, Jess," Elizabeth interrupted quickly. "I'll show you how to play some games on the computer."

Jessica mulled this one over for a while.

Then she announced brightly, "Well, I guess that'll be OK. I mean, it's almost the twenty-first century. I better get with the future. It's got to be better than the past."

"Hey, Jess, this sounds amazing!" Elizabeth said after dinner. The twins were lying on the couches in the den, and Elizabeth was reading the newspaper while Jessica read the latest issue of *Image* magazine.

"What sounds amazing?" Jessica asked with a yawn.

"There's an article about this program called GO. It lets students spend a few months going to school and living with a family in another country. Kids can go to Australia, Sweden, France—"

"Wow!" Jessica said excitedly, grabbing the newspaper from Elizabeth's hands. "This sounds fantastic! We could go to school in Paris! Just imagine it, Lizzie!"

"It would be great, wouldn't it?"

"Let's sign up right away," Jessica said. "Let's go ask Mom and Dad."

Elizabeth laughed. "Wait a minute, Jess.

Shouldn't we read the details and think about it first?''

"What is there to think about?" Jessica argued. "This is just what I've always dreamed about. The GO program could change our lives!"

How will the GO program change the twins' lives? Find out in Sweet Valley Twins and Friends #60, CIAO, SWEET VALLEY!

Join Jessica and Elizabeth for
big adventure in exciting
SWEET VALLEY TWINS SUPER EDITIONS
and SWEET VALLEY TWINS CHILLERS.

☐ **#1: CLASS TRIP**   15588-1/$3.50

☐ **#2: HOLIDAY MISCHIEF**   15641-1/$3.50

☐ **#3: THE BIG CAMP SECRET**   15707-8/$3.50

☐ **#4: THE UNICORNS GO HAWAIIAN**   15948-8/$3.50

☐ **SWEET VALLEY TWINS SUPER SUMMER**
  FUN BOOK by Laurie Pascal Wenk   15816-3/$3.50

Elizabeth shares her favorite summer projects &
Jessica gives you pointers on parties. Plus:
fashion tips, space to record your favorite
summer activities, quizzes, puzzles, a summer
calendar, photo album, scrapbook, address book
& more!

CHILLERS

☐ **#1: THE CHRISTMAS GHOST**   15767-1/$3.50

☐ **#2: THE GHOST IN THE GRAVEYARD**
                                              15801-5/$3.50

☐ **#3: THE CARNIVAL GHOST**   15859-7/$2.95

☐ 27567-4	DOUBLE LOVE #1	$2.95
☐ 27578-X	SECRETS #2	$2.99
☐ 27669-7	PLAYING WITH FIRE #3	$2.99
☐ 27493-7	POWER PLAY #4	$2.99
☐ 27568-2	ALL NIGHT LONG #5	$2.99
☐ 27741-3	DANGEROUS LOVE #6	$2.99
☐ 27672-7	DEAR SISTER #7	$2.99
☐ 27569-0	HEARTBREAKER #8	$2.99
☐ 27878-9	RACING HEARTS #9	$2.99
☐ 27668-9	WRONG KIND OF GIRL #10	$2.95
☐ 27941-6	TOO GOOD TO BE TRUE #11	$2.99
☐ 27755-3	WHEN LOVE DIES #12	$2.95
☐ 27877-0	KIDNAPPED #13	$2.99
☐ 27939-4	DECEPTIONS #14	$2.95
☐ 27940-5	PROMISES #15	$3.25
☐ 27431-7	RAGS TO RICHES #16	$2.95
☐ 27931-9	LOVE LETTERS #17	$2.95
☐ 27444-9	HEAD OVER HEELS #18	$2.95
☐ 27589-5	SHOWDOWN #19	$2.95
☐ 27454-6	CRASH LANDING! #20	$2.99
☐ 27566-6	RUNAWAY #21	$2.99
☐ 27952-1	TOO MUCH IN LOVE #22	$2.99
☐ 27951-3	SAY GOODBYE #23	$2.99
☐ 27492-9	MEMORIES #24	$2.99
☐ 27944-0	NOWHERE TO RUN #25	$2.99
☐ 27670-0	HOSTAGE #26	$2.95
☐ 27885-1	LOVESTRUCK #27	$2.99
☐ 28087-2	ALONE IN THE CROWD #28	$2.99

Buy them at your local bookstore or use this page to order.

Bantam Books, Dept. SVH, 2451 South Wolf Road, Des Plaines, IL 60018

Please send me the items I have checked above. I am enclosing $_____
(please add $2.50 to cover postage and handling). Send check or money
order, no cash or C.O.D.s please.

Mr/Ms _____

Address _____

City/State _____ Zip _____

SVH–3/92

Please allow four to six weeks for delivery.
Prices and availability subject to change without notice.